MY TRUTH

THEIR LIES

BEING BLACK IS NOT A CRIME

NO MORE HASHTAGS

SAY THEIR NAME

LESLIE CRAWFORD

ISBN: 978-1-7371235-5-2

Library of Congress Cataloging-in-Publication Data is available upon request.

My Truth Their Lies

Written by: Leslie Crawford

Cover Design: German Creative

Printed in the United States of America

To every Black person out there, you have a voice.

Your life matters.

Introduction

I don't care what anyone says; you can have all the black friends you want. But, when it comes down to picking a side, most white people will pick their side no matter what. Even when they see injustice with their own eyes, they will not cross the line to protect the victim. Yes, you have some that will march and carry their "Protect Black People" sign, but how many will help the victim at that moment?

I never had to worry about sides being picked because I got along with everyone and everyone got along with me. Just when I thought I could have a white best friend and not worry about racial issues, I learned I was the token black friend. My name is Aubrey Tucker, and I am a junior at Liberty Preparatory School, a private school not too far from my house. Before my life was ruined, I was getting ready to finish my junior year and start preparing for my last year of high school, and pick a college to attend. My life has never been perfect, but I believe I have a pretty dope life.

I was born and raised in the suburbs of a wealthy county in Maryland. I always got what I wanted even though I wasn't spoiled. My parents always had the luxury of buying me nice things, placing me in the best school, and providing me with a loving family. My parents met through a business transaction, a legal one. My mom, Tessa, has a lucrative accounting firm. She went to college and became a CPA, and started a business. They told me my dad was referred to her by a mutual friend. After she did his taxes, my dad being the charmer he is, asked her on a date. She said yes, and six months later, they were married. My dad, Kevin, is a chef. He has cooked food for some of the country's most powerful men and women. I never tasted anyone's food that was better than his. My mother can't even cook better than him.

About a year after my parents were married, I was born Aubrey Simone Tucker. When my parents were married, they lived inside an apartment. Around the time I was six months, my parents had a house built in a new community. My mom and dad were doing good in their field. My dad was doing private catering events and working for one of the most elite restaurants in the city. My mom's accounting firm was expanding. Everything was working out for my family. Growing up, I knew my parents loved each other. They had a weekly date night, and we had a weekly family night. Sometimes we went out, and other times, we would stay in. We traveled twice a year as a family for as long as I could remember, and my parents would go away every year for their anniversary. I always thought my parents would be together forever. Until his 'best friend' ruined our family. Before I tell you how the 'best friend' ruined our family, I will share some history of my family.

As I mentioned, my mom is an accountant, but she's also a business owner. She attended college for accounting, and as soon as she graduated, she received her first job as an accountant for a private company. After two years of working there, she realized she didn't want to work for anyone else. She was single, 23 years old, with no kids, so she stepped out on faith to start her business. My mom started her firm with a few thousand dollars in her bank account. Within a year of being in business, she received her first major contract, leading to many more. She was eventually labeled as the go-to person for accounting services. My mom was the youngest in her field on the East Coast, making boss moves. She made her first million within two years of being in business.

My mom had many clients, but her favorite one became her husband. I mean, who wouldn't want my mom. She's short, around 5'6", has light brown beautiful hazel smooth skin, has a gorgeous thick shape, and always keeps her weave on point. For her to be 41, people often ask if we're sisters because of how young she looks. Her almond-shaped eyes would have any man mesmerized. My mother is a beautiful black queen. I can see why my dad fell in love with her. They had the perfect love story.

My dad went to school to be a chef. He's two years older than my mom, but he looks good also. He's tall, dark brown like an almond bar, with a bald head. I don't think I ever remember my dad having hair. But, anyway. My dad was everything in my eyes. When he came home from work, he always picked me up, kissed me, and started playing with me before he begin doing anything else. When I started school, he always helped me with my homework and asked how school was going.

Both of my parents shared equal responsibilities in the household. Both of them cooked, even though I preferred my dad's cooking. They cleaned, attended school events and meetings, and always shared how much they loved me. I knew when I was older; that I wanted a marriage like, there's.

Madison, my dad's new wife, had been coming around for as long as I could remember. My dad said they met in college and became best friends. I never had a problem with her, but something about her always wanting to be around would bother me. I didn't realize she was annoying until I was in the sixth grade. At first, I called her Ms. Madison. Then she started insisting I call her Aunt Madison. I was young but I didn't like or want to label her as my aunt. My suspicions were right. When I was fifteen, during my sophomore year, my parents divorced because my dad cheated on my mom with Madison.

My mother never told me, but I overheard one of her conversations with Grand-Grand. Grand-Grand is my mom's mother, Janice. She told Grand-Grand; that my dad would always go to Madison when they argued. In turn, Madison would convince him that my mom didn't love him. I didn't even know my parents argued because they always kept it from me. I never even seen them mad at each other. That's why I thought they had the perfect marriage.

They were separated for two years, and I always thought things would work out, but they didn't. I always blamed Madison for my parents getting a divorce. Not even a year had passed after the divorce, and my dad married her, and they just had a baby. By the way, Madison is white. She was the first white person I disliked, and my former best friend became the first one I hated.

Since my first day in school, I attended private school. I don't even know what a public school looks like, other than driving past one. Our house is in a quiet, suburban neighborhood called Walnut Grove. The majority of the kids that live in this area attend Liberty Prep. My class is 90% white every school year, and the remaining 10% are kids of another race. Typically, it was probably two black kids in my class.

I always knew my parents had money; we weren't considered middle class. We were in the upper class, but my parents never allowed me to think I was better than anyone else, unlike the kids at my school. All of the houses in my area were at least a quarter million. If you lived in my zip code, you came from wealth. Most of the kids from school, parents were into real estate, politicians, CEOs, business owners, doctors, and lawyers, or they inherited their wealth, like Allison's mother. Allison is my former best friend. I'll get back to that later. Almost all of the white kids at my school came from wealth, and if you didn't, the snobby kids let you know. For some reason, if you were receiving financial aid, you weren't on their level.

I am one of the popular girls at school, mainly because I've been there for so long. All the teachers know me, and the younger black kids look up to me. When my life was ruined, I was the president of the Black Student Union, played softball, and was the school cross country team captain. So, I always made sure I let my presence be known. I wasn't ashamed of being black and never allowed the white kids at school to intimidate me. Honestly, they never bothered me.

People who look at me don't believe how outspoken I am about being black. I'm only 5'4", around 140 pounds on a good day, with clay color skin tone and locs that reach my chin. My locs are jet black with the tips of them colored red. When I started growing my locs during my freshman year, I made it clear to the school that I wouldn't cut them. I had heard too many stories about black kids being forced to change their hair or leave school because it wasn't appropriate, according to the school. But the administration let me and my mother know that the style I chose didn't matter to them. Even though Liberty Prep was a majority white school, the administration treated everyone fairly; it was the white students and some of the other black students I had to worry about. Allison was the only one I trusted.

Allison is my best friend, but she is the typical white girl. Let me rephrase that she was my best friend. I never thought she was racist, but Allison also didn't see the racism from other students I saw. That's where we often clashed. To avoid clashing, we tried to stay away from the topic of race. Allison's mom came from a wealthy family, but she couldn't touch any of the money. Her mom set up a trust fund for her when she turned 25. She only had to turn 25; no college or marriage was needed. Her mother believed that was the proper age to handle that type of money. Allison had three million dollars in a trust fund waiting for her. Wealth was inherited, which is why Allison and her family lived near us.

Allison was naïve. She saw the good in everyone. Allison always wanted to believe that everyone was good even though, deep down, she knew they weren't. I tried to see people like Allison did, but I'm not able to with the history of how black people are treated in this country. So, I try to keep things about race out of our conversation. We talk more about things we have in common like sports and shopping. She's on the cross-country team with me, and Allison plays ice hockey. Allison looks like the typical white girl, and everyone questions our friendship. She doesn't try to act black like some of the other white kids at my school. They try to portray what they believe black people are like, but it always looks super weird. She's 5'7", with pale white skin, which she often tans. She has long blonde hair that reaches the middle of her back. Everyone likes Allison because she's friends with me.

We have been best friends for the past five years. When Allison's parents divorced, they moved into one of the homes in our neighborhood. Allison's parents divorced when she eleven-years-old. Her dad moved to California to pursue his writing career, while Allison and her mom moved from one county to another in Maryland. On the first day of school, Allison instantly clicked with me when we sat next to each other. She was the new student, and I was the popular one.

No one expected us to become friends because we were of different races. I always hung out with the other black kids, but it was something about Allison. Who would have known we would have more in common than sports? Four years after we met, my parents were divorced. Even though we are best friends, our parents are just cool.

Allison's mother, Jennifer, is a Captain with the police department in our county. Jennifer's dad was a real estate mogul in New York for over thirty years. Her mother was a major fashion designer there. With Jennifer being the only child, she inherited everything from her parents. When her dad passed, he was worth over $15 million. Even though she came from wealth, Jennifer always desired to become a police officer. Go figure! That's what most crappy white people dream of. At 18 years old, Jennifer's father died from a heart attack. A year later, her mother passed from what most say was a 'broken heart.' Again, Jennifer inherited everything from her parents.

Everyone told Jennifer she would never have to work again, but that wasn't her dream. She sold every property her dad had in New York except for one. She let a relative stay in that Brownstone. Jennifer took her mom's design portfolio and sold it. The house she grew up in New York was sold, and Jennifer took her money and moved to Maryland with her new boyfriend, who ended up being her husband, Peter. They got married, he signed a pre-nub, and years later, they had Allison. When she moved to Maryland, she immediately joined the police force. Once that divorce was over, they became our neighbors.

Even though our parents weren't friends, I loved Allison and her mom. Her mom was cool, but who would have known I was just another nappy-headed black girl in their eyes when it came down to it. This happens when you trust white people who don't have your best interest at heart. All of that "I have black friends, so I'm not a racist" means absolutely nothing when your black friend becomes the victim in front of your eyes.

Chapter 1: "The Betrayal"

"Are we going to the mall tomorrow?" I asked Allison.

"Yup! My mom is letting me use the car," Allison responded. "Did your mom say you could go to the mall?"

"Yeah! It's supposed to be my dad's weekend, but he went away with the whore he calls a wife," I answered.

"At least you see your dad. Since my dad moved to California, I have only seen him through facetime. You know every time I'm supposed to visit him, his schedule changes."

"I rather not go to my dad's house. I don't like his wife," I admitted.

"I always thought she was nice, but what do I know?" Allison joked.

"His wife, Madison, is nothing but a trick. She is a prime example of why men and women shouldn't be best friends. They claimed they had been best friends since college. I know every time my dad and mom had problems, my dad talked to her, and she convinced him to leave her. So now, all of a sudden, she doesn't work. She wants to be a stay-at-home mom. She just wants his money."

"They did just have a baby," Allison added, trying to soothe the problem.

"I don't care. Let's change the subject because I don't like talking about her."

"Okay! Did you see Jeffrey in school today? He is so cute," Allison expressed.

"You know I don't like him. There is nothing about him that I like," I replied. Allison knew how I felt about that jerk, but she thinks he's the best thing out there when it comes to teenage boys.

"I know you don't like him, but I think he's cute."

"He is cute, but he's also a racist," I reminded my best friend.

"I don't think he is. It's his father that's racist."

"If his father is one and he acts just like his father, then he's a racist also. I know you hear the stuff he says, the supposed to be jokes."

"Aubrey, he was dating Kenya last school year, and she's black."

"Allison, that doesn't mean anything. Kenya was never allowed in his house, and she said the only time they were together was in school or at her house. He always came over to her house, but they never went anywhere in public or to his house. As soon as they broke up and he started dating Rebecca, she was posted all over his social media page, she's been in his house, and their parents hang out together. We both know why."

"He has never been racist towards me," Allison stated.

"Of course, you're white," I said sarcastically.

"Okay! I don't want to argue about this because we're good. There's no racism over here."

"Yeah, I have to go anyway because I was supposed to have started setting the table for dinner, and my mom will be here shortly."

"Okay, I will see you tomorrow. I'll call you later tonight if my mom is not trying to have a bonding moment."

When I got off the phone with Allison, I started preparing the table for dinner. My mom is a stickler about having the table set before putting dinner on it. The plates and utensils have to be placed a certain way. It had to be this way even if we were eating carryout. It was Friday which means we most likely were having carryout. Since my dad left, Friday nights have been made for eating out. When my mom walks through the door, she'll have the food in her hand and expect the table to be set.

After I sat the table, I knew I only had a short time window to call Jason. Jason is my boyfriend that my parents don't know about. My dad still thinks I'm too young to date. And because my parents like to be on the same page when it comes to me, my mom agreed. Which meant I went to my junior prom with Allison. Our prom was three weeks ago, and since she didn't have a date, we went together. Surprisingly, a lot of girls either came alone or with their friends.

I met Jason earlier this year. He recently transferred to our school, which was unusual in the middle of the school year. But Jason's dad is a plastic surgeon, and he made a large donation to the school, from what I heard. I also heard he was expelled from his other private school for smoking weed. So, I guess Liberty Prep let the rules slide because of the donation. Plus, what could they say when most white boys here smoke and sell weed? Jason and I have two classes together, but he made his move when we were paired up for a science project.

I told him I wasn't allowed to date, but he persisted. Finally, we promised each other that we wouldn't go to the prom with anyone else. So, he came alone, and I was with my girl. I know Jason made a mistake by smoking weed, and my parents wouldn't like it, but he's a good person. He gets good grades and is very nice to me. Everyone knows about us except for my parents. I hope my parents will change their minds when

I become a senior. So, I call Jason in the small window of time from after school until my mom gets home. Other than that, we chat in school or via text messages. Lucky for me, my mom doesn't check my phone.

"I was wondering if you would call me," Jason said before saying hello.

"Dag, no hello or nothing."

"I knew it was you. Are you still coming to the mall tomorrow?"

The mall was our way of spending time together outside of school. "Yeah, I will be there. I hear my mother pulling into the garage; I will text you."

"Ard, bye."

I hated lying and sneaking around, but what else could I do? I did tell myself; that I would talk to my parents again about dating once the school year was over.

"Hey Ma, how was work?"

"Hey, Aubrey. Work was stressful and busy. You know, once April 15th is gone, it gets even busier for those who waited to file after the deadline. I signed up for this, so I will be working from home this weekend."

"Ma, you never work on the weekend."

"I know, but this account is major, and the IRS is auditing them. We have an appointment on Monday morning, and I want to ensure I have everything in order. Plus, I am trying to get this contract with a school district to have my firm do their accounting services."

"That's major."

"How was school today? I bought some wings and a salad from that restaurant in the shopping center that you love. I got a mixture of the cinnamon, mild, and old bay with a salad."

"Thanks, Ma. We don't have any homework for the weekend because of our finals next week. We have three weeks left, and I can't wait. I wanted to know if I could work for you this summer to make some extra money. You know how you usually hire an intern? I figured you could hire me instead. I could clean up, do some data entry, run errands, or whatever you need me to do."

"I do think it's time for you to start working and making your own money. Let me think about it, and I will let you know before school lets out. I'm going to wash my hands so we can sit down and eat."

***

"Ma, I am about to leave for the mall."

"Aubrey, are you walking to Allison's house, or will her mom be picking you up?" my mom yelled from her office. I swear sometimes she has the worst memory. Of course, I told her the plans this morning, but that's how she gets during this time of the year.

"I am walking to Aubrey's house, and she is driving to the mall. Her mom is letting her use the car. I will call you as soon as I get to her house."

"Okay, be safe, and I love you."

"I love you too."

Allison lived about five to seven minutes from the house when I walked. My family was one of the first families to move into this development. Today, only three other families, including ours, were the original buyers when the homes were first built. That's according to my mother. Even though I have been living here for 16 years and my mom pretty much knows everyone around here, I still get the crazy stares from certain neighbors when I walk around alone.

There are a lot of houses around here, but they are pretty spaced out, making my walk to Allison's house seem longer than it is. When I reached Allison's house, I saw her mom's car parked in front of the house instead of in the driveway or garage. Her mom does that because Allison hit the mailbox the first time she backed out of the driveway. The smart solution would have been to teach her how to back out properly, but what do I know. So instead of going into her house, I sat on the curb near the car. I sent Allison a text letting her know I was outside. Allison responded to tell me she was in the living room putting on her shoes and was coming out.

I didn't mind sitting outside because it was a nice spring day. The sun was shining, and there was a slight breeze, but it wasn't cold. So, to me, it was another normal day until they came. I was sitting on the curb strolling through social media and saw a cop coming toward me. I didn't want them to bother me, so I stood up and started walking toward Allison's front door. As I walked, I immediately heard the sirens and someone on what sounded like they were using a bullhorn.

"Stop right there," a female voice demanded.

I knew what should and should not be done. I stood in the same spot and was barely breathing. I was terrified, trying to remember everything my parents had taught me. I shouldn't make any sudden movements, especially since my back was turned to them. I had my purse on my shoulders, so I slowly raised my hands as if I was about to be arrested. I looked toward Allison's living room window to see if she was there, but I didn't see her.

"Turn around and slowly lower your hands," the female voice continued.

I was at the beginning of the driveway as I turned around. I kept my hands raised because I didn't want to be another hashtag. My mother wouldn't be able to handle that. As I stood there with my hands raised, my heart started pounding, and it felt like my legs wanted to shake, but I was scared to move. Finally, the female officer started walking toward me. As she walked toward me, an old, fat, white officer got out of the passenger side of the police car. He leaned against the cruiser as if he were about to watch a street fight. She got close to me, so close that I could smell her lunch on her breath. It smelled like day-old Chinese food.

"What are you doing in this neighborhood?"

"I live in Walnut Grove. My house is about five minutes away from here, and I was visiting my friend who lives here," I responded. I wanted to give them as much information as possible, but I didn't want to ramble on. I knew it would make me look nervous, which would make them nervous. Anyone being nervous is a reason for them to shoot. I stared at the female officer and noted her name and badge number. Her name was Officer Cooper, and her badge number was 4836. I have a very good memory, so I know it wouldn't be hard to remember everything if I made it out of the situation alive.

Before Officer Cooper could respond, her partner walked toward us and started running his mouth. "My partner asked you a question, and she expects the truth. What are you doing in this neighborhood? I know your kind doesn't live around here."

As he got closer to me with his big stomach hanging over his pants, I read his badge number and name to myself. He was sloppy, but I knew what I needed to know. His name was

Brickley, and his badge number was 4732. "Officer, I do live around here. I have my ID in my purse, which will prove where I live. Is it okay if I lower my hands and show you my ID?" At this point, I never lowered my hands.

"No, you cannot get your ID. Cooper, take her bag and check her ID," Brickley yelled.

I didn't even get a chance to lower my arms before Officer Cooper yanked my arms down and snatched my purse off my shoulder. She opened my purse and dumped everything on the ground. After everything was on the ground, she picked up my wallet and went through it. I wanted to pull my cell phone out of my back pocket, but I knew what would happen. Someone had to be recording what was going on. I was hoping someone was.

"Here's her ID," Officer Cooper stated as she handed it to her partner.

"This doesn't say where you live. This is only a school ID."

"I attend Liberty Prep which is a private school in the area. I promise you, I live around here. You can take my phone and call my mom. She's at home right now."

"I don't want to call your mother. What are you doing in this neighborhood, sitting in front of a police captain's house? We received word that some thugs who don't live here have been hanging out. Are you walking through here casing out the joint so you can send word back to your dope-dealing friends? I know what your kind does. You see a nice neighborhood with big homes and think you can rob them. Were you watching to see when someone left their house?"

"None of that is true. I live around here. I have lived in the same house all of my life. You may know my mom. Her name is Tessa

Tucker; she has done a lot for the community. Trust me, if you call her, she will tell you. My best friend lives in this house. Her mother is Jennifer, who is the captain you spoke about. I go to school with her daughter. If you knock on the door, my best friend Allison will tell you I was waiting for her. We were on our way to the mall," I said as I started to cry. I knew deep down none of this was going to end well. I would be happy if I could make it out of this alive. I just wanted to live. As I stood in the same spot praying, Brickley opened his big mouth again.

"Cooper, you are in charge here. Are you going to let this black, nappy-headed nigger speak to you that way?"

Cooper stood there as if she didn't know what to do. I was praying that she didn't listen to him and turned away. But then, on the other hand, if something were going to happen to me, I would rather it be done by her instead of him. Before I could say anything else, Officer Cooper punched me in the face. She hit me so hard that I fell to the ground. Then, before I could get up, she kicked me in the stomach. I was in so much pain that I couldn't even block her kicks. I remember seeing some black boots going into my stomach repeatedly.

"Get her ass up and slap the cuffs on her," I heard Brickley demand.

"What are we charging her with?"

"Trespassing, Cooper."

I knew Cooper didn't want to do any of this. She pulled me off the ground, and as I stood up, I looked toward Allison's house and saw her looking out the window. She saw everything and didn't bother to help me. I looked Allison in the eyes and pleaded with her by saying, "please help me," without making a sound. I know Allison read my lips, but she didn't move. This was when I realized I was the token black friend.

Cooper placed the handcuffs on my wrist and dragged me to the car by my arm. I could barely walk, but I had to so I wouldn't be dragged on the ground. Once I reached the back of the car, Cooper threw me in, and honestly, it was a moment of relief. After that, I knew everything was over. When Cooper shut the door, I heard voices outside the car, but I couldn't determine what was said. Tears ran down my cheeks as I pleaded with God that he would get me out of this situation. Then the door opened, and Cooper leaned toward me and started punching me in my face repeatedly. After her fist became tired, she took out her baton and started hitting me as I lay on my side. I tried to ball up into a fetal position to avoid the hits, but it didn't help. Before I knew it, I was unconscious. The rest of the story is what I found out months later.

"Brickley, I think we need to call an ambulance. She's unconscious. What should I do?"

"Calm down, rookie. Do you have on your camera?"

"I didn't turn it on when we left the station. I forget sometimes."

"Good. We'll report that she assaulted you and resisted arrest. Call an ambulance, and I'll write up the report when we return to the station," Brickley ordered.

"Brickley, someone is standing on the porch across the street. What if they saw everything?"

"Please, no one will say anything to help a nigger out. That lady is white, and she'll always be on our side. I'm sure the cell phones would be recording if we were in a different area. But, lucky for us, we patrol a quiet, white neighborhood."

When the ambulance showed up, Cooper removed the cuffs. I was awake by now, but I kept my eyes closed because I didn't want them to know I was conscious. I was placed in the ambulance, and Cooper rode in the back with me. Her partner drove behind the ambulance as we made our way to the hospital. I would peek at Cooper as we were going to the hospital, and I could see the fear in her eyes. I didn't feel sorry for that dirty cop. She's going to get everything she deserves.

When I arrived at the hospital, I was given some medicine to numb the pain and placed inside a room. I wanted my mom so bad, but I couldn't talk. The only thing I could do was cry. I was in so much pain that I didn't even feel the tears rolling down my cheeks. While I was in the hospital, my best friend covered her tracks.

"Hey Allison, are you at the mall yet?"

"Ma, please help me!" Allison cried.

"Allison, what is wrong? What happened?"

"It's Aubrey…"

"What happened to Aubrey?"

"Come home, please; they beat her and took her away…."

"Allison, slow down. Who are they?"

"Please, come home."

"I'm on my way. Don't go anywhere."

While Jennifer ran home to her distressed daughter, Allison went to her driveway and retrieved some of my stuff. The cops picked up my wallet, but they didn't get everything. My cell phone, purse, and everything else were left on the ground. Allison ran outside and brought everything inside of her house. As she was covering her tracks, my mom was looking for me. My mom later told everyone that she called my phone over twenty times because I never let her know I had arrived at Allison's house. Just as I was about to text her, the cops pulled up. What Allison didn't know was my mom always knew where I was. She saw that my cell phone was at Allison's house.

"Allison, what happened?" Jennifer asked as she ran into her house.

"I don't know how it started, but the cops were talking to Aubrey outside the house. Then I saw one of them hit her, and the next thing I knew, she was thrown in the back of the police car. I couldn't see what was happening, but she was taken away in the ambulance."

"Did they see you?"

"No, I don't think they saw me, but I believe Aubrey saw me. After I got off the phone with you, I went outside and brought her stuff inside. Should I call Ms. Tessa?" Allison cried her fake tears.

"No, do not call anyone. I will call the station to see who was assigned to this area."

Jennifer called her desk sergeant and found out who the officers were. She already knew things weren't looking good.

"I found out who the officers were. One is a rookie, and the other one is a pain in my ass. Was one of them a heavy-set white man?"

"Yes."

"That's Brickley. Aubrey was dropped off at the hospital, and both officers are back on the street. You stay here. Do not answer your phone or the door. The only person you should be talking to is me. Give me her stuff. I'm going to the hospital to see what I can find out."

While I was waiting for surgery, the hospital called my mom. As I lay in the bed with only a curtain covering me, I could hear my mom in the hallway calling for me. I wanted to yell out to let her know where I was, but I couldn't open my mouth.

"AUBREY. AUBREY."

"Excuse me, ma'am, how can I help you?"

"Someone called and said my daughter was admitted here. Her name is Aubrey Tucker. Can you help me?"

"Hey, Tessa," Jennifer called out from behind my mother.

"What are you doing here? Where is Aubrey? The last I checked, she was at your house. What happened?"

"Tessa, I don't know, but I was here for another call. I just saw you and wondered if I could help. Aubrey was never at my house. I called Allison to see if they had made it to the mall, but she told me Aubrey never showed up."

"You're a damn liar. I tracked Aubrey's phone to your house. I don't know what you or your daughter have to do with this, but I will find out. But, right now, get the hell out of my face. Nurse, can you tell me where my daughter is?"

"Yes, ma'am. Follow me. I will take you to your daughter's room and get the doctor."

When the nurse pulled my curtain back, I saw my mom's face. I knew she wasn't happy with what she saw. I still hadn't seen my face, so I didn't know what she was looking at. Then, tears started strolling down her face, and she ran toward me.

"Aubrey, baby, what happened? Who did this to you?"

I couldn't say anything or move any part of my body to communicate with my mom. The only thing I could do was cry. The doctor walked in behind my mother about a minute later.

"Hi, I'm Dr. Chambers. How are you? Are you Aubrey's mom?"

"Yes, I am. My name is Tessa. What happened?"

"I don't know the complete story. My front desk nurse told me; that two officers had brought her in. The report stated she was found beaten in Forestville Shopping Center. My EMT's report was different. They found her in the back of a cruiser. I don't know which one is the truth. My primary goal right now is to help her."

"I will get to the bottom of what happened later. Right now, can you tell me her condition and what needs to be done?"

"Aubrey has bruises all over her upper body. She cannot speak because her jaw is broken. I will need to do surgery. After the surgery, her jaw will be wired shut while it heals. Her arm is broken, and she will need surgery for that also. The bruising to her abdomen, back, and face will heal on its own. I can tell you she will go through weeks of being in pain and recuperating, but she will get through this. I want to get her into surgery as soon as possible. I need you to sign some paperwork," Dr. Chambers explained as my mother stood there crying.

"How long will the surgery take?"

"Several hours, but I will take care of her. I will perform the surgery on her jaw, and then Dr. Sanders will perform the surgery on her arm."

"Where is this, Dr. Sanders? How good is he or she?"

"Dr. Sanders is finishing up with a patient, and it's a she. She is the best at the hospital. Don't worry; we will take care of her. I will have the nurse come in and prep her. I will get the O.R ready, and we will be ready in about an hour. Aubrey, we will take care of you."

I heard everything the doctor told my mom, but it wasn't something I was ready to hear. I don't know what I looked like, and from the medication they gave me, my body was completely numb. I couldn't move anything above my waist. I was lying there watching my mother try to hold it together as she calls my father. From the looks of it and some of the words, she's not happy.

"I don't care what you're doing. You need to drop everything and make your way to the hospital. That's the last thing I'm going to say."

"Aubrey, I don't know what happened, but I will find out who did this to you. Right now, I want to focus on you getting better. Don't worry about anything. I will be here when you come out of surgery."

My mother stood next to my bed with tears in her eyes. Her tears caused me to have tears of my own. I didn't want to do anything but hug her. I wanted my mother to wrap her arms around me and tell me all of this was a nightmare. My mother started running her hands through my locs as her tears dripped onto my forehead. As she stood there crying, the nurse prepared me for surgery. While the nurse was talking, I only heard mumbled words. None of what she was saying made any sense. I heard her voice and my mother's voice. I'm sure she was talking to my mother. She asked my mom many questions, took some tests, and did something to the machine I was hooked up to.

"I will be back in about 10 minutes to help the transport team take Aubrey to surgery," the nurse explained.

***

I woke up to my mom on the phone talking to someone at the company. I'm assuming it was Mrs. Kathy. Mrs. Kathy is my mom's right hand. She's an accountant, and when my mother takes a vacation, Mrs. Kathy runs the business. I don't know how long I had been out, but it was still daytime outside. Or was it the next morning?

A horrific pain shot through my body as I tried to sit up. I looked down, and my arm was in a cast; something was wrapped around my stomach, and I couldn't feel my face. My mom had her back turned to me so she couldn't see me trying to get her attention. I was in pain.

"MMMMMMMMM," I tried to scream as loud as I could.

"Kathy, I will call you back. Aubrey is awake."

"Aubrey, hey, your surgery was successful. How are you feeling?"

"Mmmmmm."

"I'm sorry, I forgot you can't speak. I will see if I can find the doctor so he can explain everything to you."

Dr. Chambers walked in just as my mother walked out of the room.

"Hi, Dr. Chambers. I was about to ask for you. Aubrey just woke up. Since she can't talk, I don't know how to help her communicate."

"Good morning, Mrs. Tucker and Aubrey…."

"You can call me Tessa or Tess. Either one is fine. But my friends call me Tess." I swear, I think my mom is flirting with my doctor.

"Tess," Dr. Chambers laughed while blushing. "Aubrey, your surgery was a success. Your jaw will be wired shut for about six to eight weeks. During this time, we need your bones to heal properly. It won't be easy to talk and eat, but I still want you to try. For the first couple of days, don't try to talk. I rather you use a tablet, or something like that to communicate with. You will start with a liquid diet. Because it will be a liquid diet, I would like you to eat five to six times a day. You can mix vegetables and fruit in a blender and sip them through a straw. You can also try Ensure, whatever your taste bud's desire. It would help if you didn't try eating food that requires chewing for at least three months or until the therapist you will see clears you. Your cast will remain on for about six to eight weeks also. Do not try to push, lift, or pull anything. Give your body time to heal...."

As Dr. Chambers explained everything, I pointed to my stomach with my left hand.

"Yes, we wrapped your stomach because of the bruising. It'll be removed before you are released. The bruising on your face, back, and stomach will heal on its own. Within one to two weeks, I would like you to start physical therapy for your jaw and arm. I will give your mom some recommendations on a physical therapist. Each of these places will allow you to do therapy on both. I know they will tell you this, but don't try to overdo it. Take your time and allow the healing to happen on its own. The nurse will come in and run some tests. You can be released today if all of your tests come back good. Do you have any questions?"

I shook my head yes. Dr. Chambers pulled out his tablet and sat it in front of me. I typed, 'what day is it?'

"Aubrey, it's Sunday. You came in yesterday, and you slept through the night. Are you hungry or in any pain?"

I typed, "no food but yes to the pain."

"I will have the nurse come in and give you some medicine, but you will have to eat something. I will have the cafeteria bring an Ensure to drink before receiving the medication. Is there anything else you need?"

I shook my head no and closed my eyes. I was already over this entire situation.

"Mrs. Tucker, I'm sorry, Tess. Did you have any questions for me?"

"Yes, what about a follow-up appointment with you?" my mom asked as her cheeks turned bright red.

"I will need to see Aubrey in a week. If there are no issues with her test, when the nurse discharges her, she'll set up her follow-up appointment."

"Thank you! If I have any questions, is there a way to contact you? Is there a number, or should I call the hospital? Of course, the questions will be about Aubrey."

I can't believe she is flirting with my doctor. He is cute and she has been single for some time now, but she is bold.

"Yes, here is my card. You can call at any time."

"Are you sure? I wouldn't want your wife to get upset, especially if I need to call in the middle of the night. I never had to deal with anything like this, so I don't know if Aubrey will have an emergency late at night."

"There is no wife or anyone else. That's my number on the card; you can call any time. Don't worry about Aubrey. She will recover well."

"Thank you. One last question, Dr. Chambers. Did you ever find out more information about when Aubrey was brought in?

Unfortunately, I haven't been able to speak with anyone about it."

"I will have the nurse bring a copy of the EMT's report and the officer's report to you. Let me know if you need anything else."

"Aubrey, hopefully, you'll be able to go home today. I will be working from home until you can get around independently. Tomorrow, I will go to the school and get your work. School will be over in less than a month, so there's no need to return. I'm going to have your teachers email me your work daily. What do you think about staying in the guest room downstairs? I think it's best so you won't have to walk up and down the stairs for the bathroom."

I hunched my shoulders because I didn't care. I wanted to go home.

"I know none of this is normal, but Aubrey, I will find out what happened to you. I know Allison had something to do with this. I don't know what happened from when you left home until you met up with her. I haven't spoken to Allison yet, but Jennifer was here when I arrived yesterday. I thought that was pretty strange. Right now, my focus is to get you home, but I will circle back around what happened."

I signaled to my mom that I wanted to say something. She pulled out her phone and opened the notepad app. I typed out, "the cops did this in front of her house."

I knew the look in my mom's eyes. She was pissed. This was the look she had when she was mad at my dad. My mom took her phone back and sat in the chair next to my bed. I don't know what she was typing, but I could tell; it was filled with anger. The nurse came in with my food drink as my mom did her thing.

"Hi Aubrey, this is your breakfast. I don't know if you need to, but I want you to try and use the bathroom. I'm going to help you go, and then we'll run some tests and see if you can go home."

I hated not being able to talk. Before I got out of bed, I asked the nurse for something to write with. She pulled out her tablet for me. "When can I get some medicine?"

"Once you return from the bathroom, you can drink your shake. After the test, I will give you some medicine."

***

It was finally time for me to go home. I looked at the clock on the television, and it was after six. The nurse went to get the wheelchair so we could leave. My mom went home earlier to get me some clean clothes. I was hoping she would throw away the clothes I had on, but she said it was needed for evidence. The nurse brought them back to me inside a clear plastic bag. I was just happy to go home finally.

Chapter 2: "The Aftermath"

"Ma, I just pulled up to the house. Please don't tell anyone about what's going on. I don't need people to start running their mouth and messing stuff up," my mom told Grand-Grand through the truck speaker.

"Tessa, I didn't say anything to anyone about what happened. But you have to understand everyone will start finding out. I don't think the family will like finding out what happened from the social place."

"What are you talking about? What is the social place?"

"You know the thing on these kids' phones where they be looking at videos."

"Social media? Honestly, I don't care how they feel. Right now, this is between her dad and us. I have to go. I need to help her out of the truck and settle in the house.

"Do you need me to come to stay with you to help out?"

"I will be working from home, so I think we'll be okay."

"Alright, Tessa, call me later."

My mom gathered my stuff from the back seat and her purse and helped me out of the car and into the house. Somehow, the things left in Allison's driveway made their way to the hospital with my wallet. When the nurse brought me my bag of clothes, my phone, and everything else in my purse were in the bag. I know they only took my wallet before taking me to the hospital. I want to tell my mother everything that happened, but I also want to lay in a comfortable bed for now and try to forget the past 24 hours.

"Sweetheart, I am going to get your stuff out of your room and bring it downstairs. Are you hungry? I have some fruit. I can make you a smoothie."

I shook my head yes and laid on the couch. I could get used to my mom waiting on me, but this pain is not in my plans. First, I wanted to speak with Allison to find out why she stood there, but on the way home, my mom made it clear that I shouldn't talk to her. As I was trying to get comfortable on the couch, someone rang the doorbell while my mom was upstairs gathering my stuff. As soon as I attempted to get up, my mother came running down the steps.

"Aubrey, I got it. You don't need to be up."

"Oh, so you finally decided to bring your ass to see your daughter?" my mom said as soon as she opened the door.

"Tessa, not right now. Can I come in, please?" I heard my dad ask from the porch.

"Sure," my mom stated as she cracked the door just enough for my dad to slide in.

"Where were you? I told you about what happened to her yesterday. You should have been at the hospital yesterday."

"I told you we were out of town."

"Out of town, my ass. This was your weekend with her. If you didn't decide to take that whore out of town, none of this would have happened. Why would you plan a getaway on a weekend when you're supposed to have your daughter?"

"Madison booked the trip months ago without checking with me. I didn't know she booked it during my weekend until I told you'll last month."

"Whatever. Your daughter is right there; talk to her," my mom said as she walked into the kitchen.

"Hey baby girl, how are you feeling?"

I looked at my dad and sighed. I think he realized that I wasn't able to talk. If he didn't, my mom let him know as she yelled from the kitchen.

"She can't talk. Her jaw is wired shut."

"Tessa, can you come here and tell me what happened?"

"I will explain everything to you after I make her dinner."

My dad sat beside me, and I laid my head on his shoulder. I'm still mad at him for everything he did, but I love my dad so much. I love him, even more when Madison isn't around. I can't stand her. As I laid in my dad's arms, I realized how much comfort he brought me. It was as if he made everything better through his presence.

"Here, Aubrey, this is strawberry and banana. I will go to the grocery store in the morning to get more ingredients."

"Why didn't you ask me to stop at the store?" my dad questioned. This was a mistake. I already know what was about to happen. Even though their marriage has been over for a while, my mom is still hurt and angry with him.

"I didn't know you were coming over here. You popped up at my house unannounced as if this is still your home. I thought you bought a brand-new condo downtown."

"Tessa, I came here as soon as I dropped Madison off. I didn't even pick up Maddox from Madison's mom's house. I had Madison go. And this is my house."

"First, it's Madison's job to pick her son up from her mother's house. Second, this is my house. When you decided to leave your family, your name was taken off of my deed."

"Do we have to do this in front of Aubrey? I want to know what happened."

"I don't know what happened. She left here Saturday afternoon to go to the mall with Allison. You know Aubrey is very responsible. She always lets me know when she gets to her destination. After about 30 minutes had passed, I didn't hear from her. I was calling and texting, but I didn't receive a response. I figured maybe her phone had died. The next thing I knew, I was getting a call from the hospital. I tracked her phone, and it was at Allison's house the entire time until it ended up at the hospital. When I got there, Jennifer was there. She told me the only reason she was there was for a call. I didn't believe her. I knew something happened to Aubrey while she was at Allison's house. When I got to her room and saw her, my suspicions were confirmed. The doctor gave me the report from the EMT and the report from the police. They were two different reports. Also, Aubrey typed this into my phone."

"The cops did this in front of her house." my dad read. "What the fuck? Cops? Where is Allison? Have you talked to her?"

"I haven't spoken to her, and I'm not. I want Aubrey to rest for a couple of days. Then, once she has some strength back, I want her to let me know what happened. She said the cops did this, so I will be getting a lawyer."

"You hear about this happening to other families, but I didn't think this would happen to my daughter."

"Kevin, please don't tell anyone what happened. I want to speak with the lawyer first to see how this should play out."

"I'm not going to say anything."

"That means to Madison also," my mom added.

"She's my wife. I already told her Aubrey was in the hospital. So, I'm not going to lie to her."

"I didn't ask you to lie to her. I asked you not to tell her. I know she's your wife, and this has nothing to do with how I feel about her. I need everything to stay on the low until we find out how to move. Please help me out."

"Okay, I won't say anything to her. What do you need help with? Do you need me to come by when I'm off to help out? Do you need food? Can I go to the grocery store? Does she have to go to therapy? I can take her to appointments," my dad asked as if he couldn't stop talking.

"I will be working from home for about a week for now. But you're more than welcome to come over whenever to help out. Just call first. I planned on going to the grocery store in the morning. As far as her therapy and doctor appointments, I will text them to you."

"Send me the grocery list, and I'll go now. There's no need for you to leave out in the morning if you don't have to.

This is what I loved about my parents. Moments like these are what I miss. When they were able to talk and get along without all the arguing and blaming each other for the past. My dad kissed me on the forehead and left for the store. Once my dad left, I stretched out on the couch and started watching television.

"Aubrey, do you want to put on your pajamas and get in the bed so you can be comfortable?"

I shook my head no. I wanted to stay there until my dad came back. I was tired and wanted to sleep, but I wanted to see my dad even more. About an hour passed, and my dad returned with bags of groceries. I know my mom didn't ask him to get all of that. But I could see his favorite snacks and other foods in the bag. This made it official. I knew he would be here on a regular basis.

My dad went into the kitchen and cooked my mom some Crab Chesapeake stir fry. I know this made her happy. He also fixed all of my smoothies for tomorrow. While I stretched out on the couch, lying on my dad's lap, my mom sat across us in his favorite chair. They both ate and talked about everything other than my situation. I was over that conversation for one day.

"Do you remember when we took Aubrey to Disney World for the first time? She loved watching Mickey Mouse on television. So, we thought she would be excited to see him in person. But, oh, she was scared out of her mind. Aubrey wouldn't go near them," my dad described as if I wasn't laying right there.

My mother started laughing so hard. It wasn't that funny. I remember that trip, and those characters scared the crap out of me. Even though I was scared at that moment, I was laughing inside. I missed my family being together. We took vacations multiple times a year. We went during spring and summer break for Christmas and other random trips. Every year we boarded a plane on December 26th. I had stamps on my passport before I was ten years old. Most of the adults in my family don't even have a passport. I wish my parents would get back together.

"Kevin, how about the vacation we took to the Maldives for our tenth anniversary?"

"I do remember that trip. It was one of our best anniversary trips."

Suddenly, the room was silent. They sat there staring at each other until my mother came out of her trance.

"It's getting late; Kevin and I need to get up early. So even though I'm not going into the office, I want to start work early. Plus, Aubrey will be falling asleep soon. I'm pretty sure she will be asking for her pain meds."

"Alright. I have to work the early shift tomorrow, but I can stop by in the evening if that's okay."

"That's fine with me. We will be here. Thank you for the groceries and cooking," my mom stated with a seductive look in her eyes. This was a different look from what she gave the doctor earlier today. My mom still loved my dad.

My dad kissed me on my forehead again, told me he loved me and left. My mom helped me take a bath and put on my pajamas. I was finally in bed and ready to relax for the rest of the night. I turned my cell phone back on, and there were over 100 texts and phone calls from Allison. The battery in my phone died from it being on while the hospital had it with my clothes. It's been on the charger since we came home. I wanted to talk to Allison, but I couldn't. Most of her messages asked if I was okay and could call her.

I scrolled through my social media page, wondering if there was any word about what happened to me. Nothing. Zip. Zada. I guess no one cared about the wealthy black girl with locs being beat. Finally, I looked at Allison's page, and she had posted pictures as if she didn't stand there and watch me get the shit punched out of me. There were pictures of her, Jennifer, and her step-father David at the beach. I don't know if they were old pictures or if they went while I was in the hospital. I couldn't believe it, but they would all get what they deserve.

***

It was three in the morning, and a sharp pain just ran through my body. I needed my medicine, but my mother left it on the dining room table. As I tried to get out of bed, my legs felt weak. I needed my mother, but I couldn't find my phone. I thought I left it on the nightstand, but it wasn't there. I felt around my bed, and it was under my pillow. I called my mom's phone, and as soon as she answered, I hung up. I was hoping she would get the picture that I needed her. And she did. A minute didn't even go by, and she was walking into my temporary room.

"What's wrong, Aubrey?"

I text her phone, "I'm in pain," with tears in my eyes.

My mother went into the kitchen and grabbed me a bottled water and my pain medicine. Because of my mouth, I had to take a liquid-style medicine. So, I drank some water and followed it up with my medicine.

"Do you want me to stay in here with you?" my mother asked me.

I shook my head no and directed my eyes towards the remote control. I figured I would watch a movie until this medicine put me to sleep. My mother handed me the remote, and I used my good hand to turn on a movie. My mother left out and went back to her room. I guess that's where she went. Not long after turning on the television, I dozed off until our doorbell kept ringing. With one eye closed and squinching the other, I looked at the nightstand clock, and it was 6:32. Who would be ringing our bell this early? I soon found out when I heard my mother fussing.

"Ma, what are you doing here this early? Aubrey probably just went back to sleep. Why didn't you tell me you were coming over? It's too early for this," my mom stated in her most agitated tone.

"Tessa, you better change that tone because I am still your mother. I knew if you were working from home today, you would need some help with Aubrey. You know I wake up early anyway. If I had called you first, you would have tried to convince me not to come. You can go into your office and do whatever work you need to do. I can take care of Aubrey," Grand-Grand demanded.

My mother knew she couldn't argue Grand-Grand down. Once she said what was on her mind, that was it. I closed my eyes and went back to sleep until Grand-Grand came into my room, opening the blinds and curtains. The sunlight from outside beamed right into my room. I already knew she was going to get on my nerves.

"Aubrey, sweetheart, wake up. I know you're dealing with a lot, but you cannot lay around all day."

"Mmmmmmmmmm," I mumbled through my wired jaw. I was rolling my eyes while they were closed. If she caught me doing it, that was my butt.

Before I could do or try to say anything else, my mother came barging into the room. I would rather stay with my dad than with these two in this house. But I already knew Grand-Grand could only stay for the day.

"Ma, leave her alone. If she wants to lay around, she can."

"Tessa, if she lays in that bed all day, her body will become stiff. I'm sure the doctor would agree that she needs to move around as much as possible."

"Wrong! Try again. The doctor told her to take it easy for the first week. Aubrey woke up in the middle of the night in pain. After that, her medication put her to sleep. So, when you decided to ring my bell early in the morning, I am pretty sure she had just gone back to sleep. It's only 9, so don't act like it's late. If you're going to be here, don't get on our nerves. Let her be until she's ready to get up."

"You better watch how you speak to me. Ya'll are so ungrateful. I come here to help, and this is how I am treated."

"You act as if you drove far. You live a good 15 minutes away. I appreciate you, and I know Aubrey does, but leave her alone. She will let you know when she needs something. Ma, please."

As those two argued about what I did or didn't need, I tried my best to go back to sleep. It didn't happen. Grand-Grand eventually walked out of my room, and my mother followed. She returned five minutes later.

"Aubrey, your headmaster sent me an email. Each of your teachers will send your work daily until school is over. The headmaster said, don't worry about finals since you're already an A student. You will have to complete each assignment for the remaining couple of weeks. Okay."

I shook my head yes and closed my eyes. Then, I heard the bedroom door shut. Shortly after that, my cell phone started chiming, alerting me to a text message. It was my dad checking on me. I ignored it and turned my phone off. I was finally able to get some sleep.

When I finally woke up, the clock said 1:08, and I was hungry. I could hear my stomach rumbling, but I hated eating or drinking anything without brushing my teeth first. How was I going to do that? I turned my phone on to text my mom. The first message I saw when my phone came on was from Jason.

"Where r u???" Jason texted.

I didn't want to lie to him, but I couldn't tell the full truth. *"Not feeling well. Stayed home."*

He responded immediately, *"I miss seeing you today."*

I responded with a smiley face emoji. Then I sent my mom a message asking about brushing my teeth. She was opening my door in less than a minute. I think I could get used to this attention.

"I forgot to tell you the doctor gave you some mouth wash. He also said to brush your teeth as normal but be gentle with it. Do you want me to brush them for you?"

I shook my head no. I had a broken arm, but I wasn't a baby. I brushed my teeth and washed my face. It seemed like it took me almost 45 minutes to get myself together. I walked into the living room, and Grand-Grand was sitting on the couch watching court shows. I slowly walked toward her, and she patted the couch for me to sit next to her.

"Baby, how are you feeling? Do you want something to eat?"

I hunched my shoulders about my feelings but shook my head aggressively to the food. Grand-Grand knew what I was saying because she started laughing. She walked into the kitchen and got my smoothie. I liked these smoothies, but I don't know how long I would drink them as a meal. This was going to be a boring healing process. I couldn't talk to anyone or do anything—what a way to end my junior year.

A couple of hours went by, and the doorbell was ringing. The only person it could have been was my dad, and that wouldn't be a good look. Grand-Grand has disliked him since my parents were separated. Any time they were in each other's presence, it was ugly. Every sarcastic remark that could be made was bound to come up. My mother came downstairs, but it was too late.

"I got it, Tessa."

"Ma, it's…."

"What is he doing here? Girl, it would help if you had told me he was coming. I would have taken my ass home. What, Madison let you out of the house?"

"Nice to see you, Janice. I see you pulled out the new wig today. Hot date afterward? Have you met husband number three yet?"

"At least I can get a husband, unlike your mother."

These two are always throwing jabs at each other. Finally, my dad walked past Grand-Grand, came to the couch, and sat next to me.

"By the way, this is my real hair. I don't have to wear a wig like your momma. And that's my seat."

"Ma and Kevin, not today. If you two cannot act civil, both of you will have to leave. Ma, you started it, and I'm stopping it."

"How are you doing, baby girl? Do you need anything?" my dad asked as I laid my head on his shoulder. I shook my head no to his question about me needing anything. My grandmother didn't want to be in the same room as my dad, so she left.

"Tessa, I'm going to go home. It looks like you have all of the help you need. If you need me to come back tomorrow, let me know."

"Bye Ma. Thanks for coming over," my mom said.

"Aubrey, I will text you later. Let me know if you need anything."

My grandmother left, and there was peace in the house again. At first, my mom was sitting in the living room with us until her work phone kept ringing. Then, finally, she went back upstairs and left us alone.

"Aubrey, tell the truth. Was that a wig your grandmother had on?" my dad said while laughing.

I wanted to laugh so bad, but my mouth was hurting. I shook my head no. Grand-Grand always had long hair. She went to the salon every two weeks to get her hair done. She made sure Kelly, her hairstylist, did a different style every time she sat in her seat.

"I'm going to take you to your follow-up appointment with your doctor on Wednesday. Your mom has an important meeting with a client."

I heard everything my dad said, but I was tired. I wanted to go back to sleep. My body was not only hurting; it was tired. So, I laid there and dozed off again.

"I didn't do anything wrong."

"Shut up, you black bitch. These black kids think they can move into our neighborhoods because their parents have money. I'm going to teach you a lesson today."

"ALLISON."

"I don't have anything to do with it, Aubrey. You put this on yourself by being in this neighborhood."

"Allison, please help me."

I woke up to my first nightmare since all of this had happened. My pillow was soaked. I touched my shirt, and that was wet also. It hurt to try and sit up, but I needed to change my shirt. I had two choices. I could do it myself or have my mom help me. I knew she would want to talk about everything if I called her. I didn't want to talk. It wasn't easy, but I was able to put on a dry shirt. Lucky for me, my mom loves pillows. There were five other pillows that were in the room. I picked up one from the chair that sat in the corner and laid back down.

The clock that sat on the nightstand was starting to become annoying. When I looked at it, the clock read 11:08. I was sure my dad was gone, and my mother was asleep or on the phone. I knew she wasn't working. My mother made sure she didn't do any work after 6:30, whether she worked from home or went into the office. I don't know how I got into my room. My goal again was to watch television until I fell asleep.

Chapter 3: "I Didn't Want This"

"Aubrey, welcome to your first day of physical therapy," my therapist Makayla greeted me.

I wanted my dad to come with me because I knew he wouldn't ask a bunch of questions. My mother is going to ask every question she can. She will want to be involved in every part of this. I know she'll eventually think the therapist's name is Tessa instead of Makayla. She will try to take over. My mother called my dad this morning and told him her meeting was canceled, and she was taking me. My dad was somewhat relieved because his restaurant had a major event that afternoon. My dad took me to my follow-up appointment last week with Dr. Chambers. The plan was for him to bring me to therapy because my mom told us she had to meet with a new client.

Makayla was the head therapist here. Her dad opened his physical therapy spot 20 years ago, and now there are five locations throughout Maryland. The best part is that it's black-owned. There are a few white employees, but I am happy to start my process with a black woman.

When I went for my follow-up appointment, I found out that I would have to see a counselor about my mental aspect and see a physical therapist. I don't think it's necessary, but my mother and her new doctor friend think it's needed.

"Aubrey, I will help you throughout this process. You'll be visiting me twice a week. I will help with your jaw healing and arm. We will also go over some mouth exercises you need to do at home. I will stretch you beyond what you want to do for your arm. It will hurt but trust me. It'll help you in the long run. Any questions?"

I shook my head no, and with my mother on my heels, we walked to the back. The room I had my session in was filled with pictures of black doctors in different fields. Everything was clean, and it smelled like disinfectant. The colors were black and silver, which made me feel at home. Our basement colors were black and silver. My mother called it her relaxation room. And that it was. I always felt at ease anytime I was down there.

After an hour of therapy, it was time to leave. My arm and jaw were hurting so bad. She had me doing all kinds of mouth exercises so my jaw wouldn't be stiff. Makayla told me to try and talk. It's been a week since everything happened, and she said I need to stop communicating by text messages. I can talk, but I'm afraid it'll hurt even more. She also suggested I start eating solid food such as mashed potatoes, soup, and other soft things. The only problem with that is, I'm not a big fan of potatoes unless they're french fries. And I hate soup unless it's cream of crab. I was also tired of smoothies. I'm sure if I text my dad what Makayla said about the food, he'll whip me up something good.

"I am going to run inside of the grocery store. Do you want anything?" my mom asked as she pulled into a parking spot.

"Can you get me some apple juice?"

"Yeah, I'll be right back."

I already knew I would be sitting in the car for at least 45 minutes. My mother cannot go into any store and come back out. So at least 20 minutes passed, and she was still inside. As I sat there, being the impatient person, I tend to be, my phone alerted me to a text message. It was Allison. I hadn't heard from her since I came home from the hospital. At first, I thought she got the hint that I didn't want to talk to her. Or she didn't know what to say and figured she would let some time go by.

"You haven't been in school. Is everything good? Allison texted.

She must have lost her mind. Did she ask me if everything was good? I wanted to respond to her so badly, but my mother told me to cut all communication. I went from typing a message to deleting it to looking out the window. I did the same thing repeatedly until I saw something, well, someone. Right away, my heart started beating so bad. I knew I was having a panic attack. My hands were shaking so badly that I dropped my phone on the floor. I started sweating, and my mother was taking too long. The last thing I needed was for them to see me. The only good thing about this situation was that mom had tints on her window. Even with the tints, I slid down into my seat to where I was almost on the floor. If we were in the Porsche, this would have hurt every part of my body.

But instead, she drove the Range today. I was balled up in a fetal position with my eyes closed. I prayed to God, asking that those cops that beat me didn't see me as they walked past the truck. I don't know how long I was on the floor, but I heard the car door open and screamed.

"Aubrey, why are you on the floor? What happened? Are you okay?" my mom asked in her panicked voice. Whenever she panicked, her voice became high-pitched.

I couldn't say anything. My panic attack was even worse once she opened the door.

"Aubrey, please talk to me. What happened? Use your words."

"I'm not a child. Don't tell me to use my words," I mumbled.

"I know you're not a child, but I can't help you if you don't tell me what's going on."

My mom placed the groceries on the back seat and walked to the truck's passenger side. She helped me up into my chair and placed my seat belt on me. Once my mother was back in the driver's seat, I told her what, well, who I saw.

"The two cops who did this to me walked past the car and went into the pizza spot," I said through the tears and snot rolling down my face.

"Here, take this napkin and clean your face. Aubrey, they cannot and will not hurt you again. This is why I keep saying you need to go to therapy. I know you don't think it's necessary, but your mental health is important. You will have to face them and other cops eventually. Clean your face and breath. Tomorrow morning, I will make an appointment to see the therapist. You're not going to battle me with this."

"But why are they still on the street?" I cried.

"I have an appointment with my lawyer friend tomorrow. I think it's best to let them think everything has blown over. We will get justice. Don't worry."

Everything my mom said went in one ear and out the other. I didn't want to hear about getting justice. No one ever gets justice. Black people don't get justice when beaten and killed by the cops. Five minutes later, we were pulling into the garage. My mom grabbed the groceries, I picked my phone up off the floor, and we walked inside the house. I went straight to the bathroom to take a hot bath. I wanted to get the scent of today off of me.

Last night my mom finally let me move back into my room. My body wasn't as sore, and I could start doing things independently. My arm and mouth were still painful to move, but my bed was more comfortable than the guest room. The guest room bed was only full-size. I am short, but I am used to my king-size bed.

After my bath, I put on some pajamas and laid on the mini couch under my window seal. This is where I did most of my thinking. My mom bought me this couch last year for Christmas. I told her I wanted somewhere I could sit in my room other than my bed. I went from my couch to the bed, back to the couch, and back to the bed more times than I could count. My pacing was interrupted by my cell phone ringing. It was Jason. I couldn't talk to him, and I knew he was getting sick and tired of me.

The last time I spoke with Jason was last week. He has been calling and texting me for the past three days. I wanted to let him know what happened, but I couldn't. If I answer him, Jason will keep asking why I haven't been in school. He will break up with me if I don't talk to him. So instead of answering the call, I sent him a text message.

"WYD," I texted.

"WYD. I have been calling you. I thought you were ghosting me," Jason responded.

"I was in an accident last week. I probably won't be back since school is over soon," I lied.

"R U OK?????"

"Yes, but I broke my arm. I will text you later tonight. About to eat."

"Miss you. Facetime me soon."

"K"

I looked at the clock, and it was only 3 o'clock. I was tired of being in this house. My mother annoyed me because she always wanted to talk about what had happened. If she wasn't talking to me, she was working. I was hoping she would go back into the office but nope. As much as I hated my dad's wife, I wanted to stay with him. I knew he wouldn't bug me all day long.

On the other hand, he would be a work, and I would be stuck with Madison. I wasn't interested in being around her all day without my father being there. Plus, their condo was too small for me. It was a nice condo in the city, but not for me. I did have my room, but it was a twin-size bed and 32-inch television. I'm not materialistic, but I'm used to what I have at home. Finally, my mother interrupted my thoughts with food.

"Aubrey, I made some garlic mash potatoes. Are you hungry?"

"Yes. Ma, Allison sent me a text message today," I confessed.

"About what? Did you respond?"

"No, I didn't respond to her. She asked me if everything was okay. When will all of this be over?"

"I don't know."

I walked past my mother without saying anything. I wanted to cry because I wished this was a nightmare. But unfortunately, this wasn't a nightmare, and if I started crying, she would start. Both of us crying isn't a good combination. As I was walking down the stairs, our doorbell rang. I didn't even bother to see who it was because I knew my mom would dart past me to answer it. My mother looked through the peephole, and from the look on her face, she wasn't happy.

My mother waved me into the dining room. Whoever was at the door, she didn't want them to see me. "What are you doing here?"

"Hi, Tessa. Allison wanted to stop by and check on Aubrey. She said she had been trying to reach her. I know she was in the hospital, but I don't know what the results were," Jennifer explained nervously.

"First of all, don't come to my house unannounced. Second, Allison doesn't need to contact or worry about my daughter. Get off my porch and make this your last time coming over here."

"Ms. Tessa, if I could just talk to Aubrey…."

Before Allison could say anything else, my mother let her have it. "Look, you will not talk to Aubrey ever again. I don't know why you thought it was okay to stand there and watch my daughter get beat by your mother's co-workers. I don't know why you thought it was okay to act as if my child is supposed to be okay. I don't know why you and your mother think it's okay to show up at my damn house and think we're supposed to open our home to you. Jennifer, take you and your daughter and get the hell off of my property."

My mother's tone was so ruthless that I was frozen on the spot. I was scared to move even though she wasn't talking to me. After she closed the front door, I peeped out the living room window and saw Allison wiping what looked to be a tear from her eyes. I guess from that conversation, I'll never hear from her again. What gives her the right to start crying? Should someone feel sorry for her? Does she expect me to feel sorry for her because my mom yelled? It's crazy how she was always welcomed into my house; now, my mother doesn't want to even lay eyes on her. Now, what's next?

***

"Aubrey, your phone is ringing?" my mom told me as she was cooking dinner.

I was sitting in the living room waiting for my dad to come by. I forgot I left my phone on the counter. I haven't been getting any calls or texts lately. So, I had no idea who was calling until I stood face to face with my mother as she held my phone in her hands.

"Who is Jason?"

I stood there staring my mother in her eyes, speechless. I didn't know what to say or how to answer that question. At sixteen, if I had to speak to my parents about a boy, I never knew what to say. I hunched my shoulders and reached out for my phone.

"Aubrey, you can talk, so don't hunch your shoulders. Who is Jason? Why does he have hearts next to his name? Why would he be calling you?" my mother questioned me as if her new career was an attorney.

"He's a friend that goes to my school. That's all," I mumbled.

"Why didn't you tell me about him? Why did you hunch your shoulders? Why are you keeping him a secret? How long has he been your 'friend'?"

"You and dad told me I couldn't date, so I was scared to say something. He goes to my school, and I like him, but I didn't want you to judge him. I thought I could talk to you about it, but sometimes you aren't open to things you don't agree with."

"Why would I judge him?" my mother continued to question. Her facial expression still hasn't changed. This was her annoyed and don't play with me face.

"He was put out of his old private school for smoking weed," I continued to mumble. I felt like my five-year-old self when I knew I had done something wrong but was scared to face my parents.

"So, he's a junkie?"

"No, it was a mistake. He told me everything."

"Either way, I don't want you talking to him. With everything about to happen, the last thing we need is for the media to find out your 'friend' was put out of school for smoking weed. You have a clean record, and no surprises are welcomed. Do you understand?" my mother drilled me like I was that five-year-old girl.

Without saying anything, I snatched my phone, rolled my eyes, and made my way to my room. At this point, I didn't even care about my dad coming. My mother can be such a hypocrite. First, she's always talking about how people need second chances. Or to never judge someone for their past. But that's exactly what she was doing with Jason. She hadn't even met him, and suddenly, he's not good enough for her daughter. Before I could shut my door, my mother's hand was on my door, pushing it back open.

"Now, I know you are going through something mentally and physically, but you better not ever snatch anything out of my hand again or roll your eyes at me. Do you understand?"

I had to choose my tone carefully, but I also wanted to get my point across. "No, I don't understand. You told me not to judge anyone, but you're judging someone you don't even know. He made a mistake, and the only thing you're worried about is your reputation. This happened to me, but you're worried about yourself."

"It's not about judging him, Aubrey. You kept a secret from your father and me. There was a reason you kept him from us. My decision is final, and you cannot see him."

"That's not fair," I stated in my firm but low tone. My mouth was starting to hurt, so I didn't want to keep talking.

"It's not fair. None of this is fair, but I'm trying to protect you and this family from what is about to happen. This should have never happened to you."

"You're right; this should have never happened to me. But did you think I was exempt? Was I supposed to be exempt because we live in this wealthy neighborhood? Should I have been exempt because 100% of the houses around here cost at least a half-million dollars? Is that why I should have been exempt? Or should I not have been targeted because you are this big prominent figure in the accounting world? You make thousands of dollars in donations, and you do so much for the community. Is that why this shouldn't have happened to me? So, if I lived in the city with Freddie Grey, it would have been, okay? Is that what you're saying to me?"

"No, Aubrey, that's not what I'm saying...."

"What are you saying? Because it did happen to me. It didn't happen to you. I didn't have a desire to wake up and become a hashtag because that's what's going to happen. I didn't want all of this pressure on my shoulders. You can only talk about how big this case will get and how they messed with the wrong family. Can you imagine what I'm going through? I can only think about how messy all of this will get. But you have the nerve to say this should have never happened to me. Why? Because we live on a street where everyone is driving a Range Rover, Bentley, a Porsche, or some other type of luxury car. Is it because you surround yourself with people that can and will only send their child to a private school? Every parent in this area can buy us kids all the designer clothes in the world, take us on luxury vacations, and leave whenever you want to block out what's happening in the world. Since you and the rest of them can do it, is that why this should have never happened to me? Tell me. You're saying this should have never happened to me. It's not supposed to happen to anyone. Not Sandra Bland, Trevon Martin, Oscar Grant, or anyone else.

"This was not in the plans to happen to anyone, but it makes me no different. I'm black just like they are. The only difference in your eyes is we have money. But, the only difference in my eyes is that I survived because they weren't bold enough to kill me. What then? What would have happened if they had killed me? I have been doing the same routine for so long. I walked to my best friend's house and nothing ever happened to me. I get the stares all the time, no matter what. No one ever bothered me. That day was different.

"You are so judgmental, and you don't even know it. Do you think things would have been different if you had bought me the car I asked for when I turned sixteen, even if I didn't have a license? Could things have been different if I got my license and was sporting a Lexus like the other rich kids around here? Nope. They would have still pulled me over once they saw a black girl with locs driving a luxury car. None of this is fair to me. I didn't want any of this. I couldn't even finish out my junior year.

"I have to go into my senior year answering or ignoring questions about what happened. It's never going to end now that it has started. I'm the one that will have the racist white kids running their mouths saying, 'I should have listened to the cops.' Or, there will be the black kids who will be scared to say something because they don't want to lose their cred with the white people. Oh, let me not forget about those that want to comfort me every day, like you. Every day you're smothering me. I can't do anything without you on my heels. If I sit on the deck, you're pulling up a chair with your laptop. If I'm sitting on the couch, you are asking if everything is okay. You don't want me going to my dad's house. Family functions are out of the question because you don't want anyone to know anything yet. When this whole thing started, the first thing you said was not to tell anyone. It had nothing to do with the case being jeopardized; it was all about your reputation. You didn't want any of this on your shoulders. What makes you think I want it on mine? I am sixteen; this is my time to enjoy life. Do you know what my future will look like? This is something I have to carry with me forever. Aubrey is going to be a hashtag, not you…."

"Aubrey, calm down."

"Don't tell me to calm down. I have the wire in my mouth. My arm is broken; my body was beaten, not yours. I have the right to be upset. I was in pain, not you. I'm still in pain as I stand here and argue with you. Everything with you was always about money and a reputation. Not one time did you or dad sit down and have a conversation with me about race. You told me what not to do, and that was it. When I come to you about issues, you always say there's not enough evidence or for me not to concern myself with it. I learned everything about racism from social media or television, not from my parents.

"This wasn't a topic discussed in the Tucker household. I educated myself on black pride, racism, and everything else. I heard the conversations you had with your friends. I heard you guys say, 'if they didn't resist arrest, it wouldn't have happened to them. They should have just kept their mouth shut. I'm sure they had something on them or were doing suspicious things for the police to stop them.' Is that what you secretly were thinking about me? I had to be doing something."

"No, Aubrey, I would never…."

"You would because if I weren't your daughter, there would have been some ignorant conversations between you and your friends. I don't want any of this. I damn sure don't want to be the brave black girl that survived a police beating. This is my time to think about college, and the only thing I can think about is what will happen during my admissions process and once I'm on campus. If I go to an HBCU, I will be known as the girl with the hashtag. Everyone will want me to join their black club to speak out about justice and what happened to me. I can be the example they are looking for. If I go to their school, everyone will feel sorry for me.

"I won't get into a white school because of my grades or being an athlete. It'll be because I went through a tragedy and have a story to tell. Every college essay will expect me to talk about. This isn't going to be only local once it gets out there. Did you think about that? My face will be all over the news. Everyone will want an interview, and you're going to jump at the chance to do them. I don't want any of this.

"Twenty years from now, my children will ask me what happened. Do you now understand I don't want this fight? I'm not looking forward to fighting this thing. Yes, I want them to pay for it, but as we know, they get away with everything, so what's the point? They are still on duty and will remain on duty. But you go ahead and get your big shot attorney so you can make an example out of them. I'll be here waiting on everything to go down. I'll do whatever you want, but I'm not going to cut Jason off. He's my friend, and you have no right to judge him."

There was nothing my mother could say because she knew I was right. She walked out of my room and closed the door behind her. I was going to stop hiding Jason from my parents. I was going to start talking to him whenever I wanted. He's going to know what happened to me. He'll probably be the only friend I have after this.

"*Sorry I missed your FT, but I was lying down. Still n pain from the accident,*" I texted Jason.

"*R we good. It seems like there is more to it than an accident.*"

"Yes, we r good. I do have to tell you something but not right now. I will FT you tonight after dinner."

Jason never responded to my last text message. It was probably over because I was afraid of disappointing my parents. I couldn't even tell him the truth. I lay in my room for the rest of the evening until I heard the doorbell ring, followed by someone knocking on my bedroom door.

"Who is it?" I whispered, knowing they wouldn't be able to hear me.

"Aubrey, are you sleeping? Are you dressed?" That was my dad. I was happy to hear his voice.

I jumped up, forgetting my arm was still in a sling. "Hey, dad."

"Your mom called me and said you were upset. I figured I would come by instead of calling. What's going on?"

"She's getting on my nerves. The only thing she does is hover over me. I can't go anywhere in this house without her trailing behind me. I can't do anything but sleep, go to appointments, eat and watch television. I can't even eat the food I want."

"What about this boy she mentioned?"

I rolled my eyes. She couldn't wait to call him and run her mouth.

"Spill it. Who is this boy?" my dad asked as he continued to pry.

"There's a boy named Jason that goes to my school. We have been talking to each other for a while. He's a nice person that comes from a great family."

"What is this about him smoking weed? We don't hang out with drug addicts."

"He smoked weed one time and got caught at his old school. It was a mistake. He doesn't smoke anymore."

"How do you know this?"

"Because I know him. I don't want to go back and forth with you about this. I already told mommy how I felt about it. He is the only friend I have right now, and I'm not going to cut him off. So, it doesn't matter what anyone says."

"Okay. If you're determined to keep seeing him, I want to meet this boy."

"How? I can't even tell anyone about what's going on. If he sees me, he'll wonder what happened. I have already been lying to him. I told him I got into a car accident."

"You know I don't condone lying, but for now, that's all he needs to know."

My dad surprised me. But he is cooler than my mom. I want him to meet Jason, but where? I know my mother will not allow him to come over here. "Where will you meet him at?"

"I can ask your mother to allow him to come over this weekend. Then, I can cook dinner, and we can get to know him."

"Thanks, but I'll pass," I said.

"Why? I thought you wanted us to meet him."

"I did, but I don't want you or mom to grill him. And I don't want him to see me like this. I only want you guys to be okay with me talking to him on the phone."

"If he likes...."

Before my dad could say anything else, I had to stop him. "It has nothing to do with if he likes me. It's not that I think he would think something bad; I don't want him coming over at this time. And you know how mommy is."

"I get it. If you two are only talking on the phone, I am fine with it. Just be careful about what you say because you know your mom wants this on the hush-hush," my dad stated as he held his pointing finger close to his mouth."

"Does that work for you?"

"Yes. Thank you. Did you bring anything over to cook, or did you cook anything today?"

"I did make you something," my dad said as he left in suspense.

"What is it?"

"I made your favorite shrimp and grits."

"Great, but I can't eat the shrimp."

"You don't have to eat the shrimp, but it has the flavor in it. You want to come downstairs and eat?"

"Yes, thanks."

For the rest of the evening, I ate and laughed with my dad. My mom was in her office working. This moment with my dad was the best time since everything had happened. After eating, I found myself lying on the couch with him. Then, we watched our favorite movie, The Great Debaters. I don't know how long we were there because I woke up at 2 am to my father trying to whisper on the phone.

"Sweetheart, I told you I fell asleep on the couch while watching a movie with Aubrey."

I don't know what was being said on the other end. According to his responses, my dad was talking to Madison. I'm sure she was upset that he was still here, and she accused him of sleeping with my mother. I pretended I was still asleep.

"Madison, Tessa is somewhere in this house. I don't know where she is or what she's doing. I was spending time with my daughter, that's going through something. We fell asleep. No one is sleeping with anyone. I am with you, not her. I'll be there shortly."

"Dad, are you leaving?" I asked as if I was just waking up.

"Yes. I have to work tomorrow, but I will call or text you. Love you. Lock the door and put the alarm on. Oh, and don't sleep down here."

"Love you too, dad."

After turning the alarm on, I made my way to my bedroom. I peeked into my mom's room, and she was knocked out sleep. Snoring and everything. She had her laptop on one side of the bed and her cell phone and work books on the other side. I was surprised she fell asleep working. I guess she needed a distraction after our argument. I love my mom so much. I know how hard she has worked to get us to where we are now. I felt bad about the way I spoke to her earlier. It was my truth. I needed to speak my truth.

***

It's been one month since everything happened to me. I have been going to physical therapy for almost a month now. Makayla told me everything was going well with my healing. If progress continues, my cast will be off within three weeks. The wire will be coming off soon. I am talking better and more. I'm still scared to eat anything other than soft food. I still hadn't facetimed Jason. I think it's over between us. I have been texting him, and his responses are really short. The one thing my mom taught me about boys is if they act like they're not interested, believe them.

My dad always told me that if a boy wants me, he'll show it. He won't ignore me or treat me differently. He'll talk to me when something is wrong. This is not like the Jason I know. I have tried calling him, but it goes to voicemail after two rings. He will not answer my calls but will respond to my text. But it's a short response. A part of me can understand why he may be mad. The other part of me doesn't understand. I guess it's over.

In other news, I will finally meet the attorney my mother hired today. I have been hearing her talk on the phone with this lady. My dad is coming over also. According to my mother, today is the day the world will hear what happened to me.

"Aubrey, your dad is here," my mother informed me from the bottom of the stairs.

I walked downstairs, and my dad was there with my little brother, Maddox. I rarely spend time with Maddox because I don't like going to their condo. He's only five months, but I should be around him more. He needs to know his sister. I love my brother, but I don't feel like he's my brother. Most likely, it's because I can't stand his mother.

"Hey, dad. Hi Maddox," I sparked up the urge to speak to both of them.

Maddox sat there in the car seat, smiling. He didn't understand anything I said, I'm sure. I need to stop treating him like the ugly stepchild because Madison is the whore.

"How are you feeling today?" my dad asked, knocking me out of my trance.

"I'm good. What's Maddox doing here?"

"Madison went to brunch with her friends. It's a daddy and son day. After we leave here, I'm taking him to Centennial Park. I know it's not much for him, but he'll enjoy a nice stroll. Do you want to go?"

"Maybe. I'll see how I feel after this meeting."

It was about 10 minutes of my dad cooing and me sitting there hoping he'd stop when the doorbell rang. My mother came bouncing into the foyer as if she was expecting a gift. I don't know too much about this lawyer. I only know she and my mom went to college together. That's it. I had never heard of her until now.

"Pam, girl, I am so happy to see you. Why did it take something like this for us to see each other?" my mom announced as soon as she opened the door.

"That's because you are over here building empires. Give me a hug."

After their embrace and acting like silly high school friends, my mom finally let her in. "Pam, this is Aubrey and my ex-husband Kevin."

"Who is this cutie?" Pam asked, not even acknowledging dad and me.

"Oh, this is Maddox. Kevin's new baby."

"He's adorable. Nice to meet you, Kevin and Aubrey. Shall we get down to business?" Pam asked.

"Yes, please. Do you want something to drink? Coffee? Tea? Water? Lemonade?"

"I'll take some water. Thank you," Pam responded.

There was something about this lady that I liked. I don't know if it was the bad suit that she had on. She wore a pair of red slacks, a black three-quarter shirt with a red and black polka dot tie. Her black five-inch red bottoms set the outfit off. She didn't have any jewelry other than her wedding ring and a pair of diamond studs. I don't know much about diamonds because jewelry is not my thing. I couldn't even guess how many carats were in her ear.

My mother always told me a woman's nails say a lot about her. I looked at her nails, and they were neatly done. Her makeup was only lipstick. Her skin was beautiful. There were no pimples or marks on her skin. I would love to know her skin regimen. It was smooth and the color of truffle. She wore her hair out in a twist-out style. It reached her shoulders. I'm pretty sure it was all her hair because it looked healthy. My mother interrupted me, admiring my new lawyer with her water.

"Here's your water. What's first?" my mom interrupted.

"I have been working on everything from my office. Before I came here, I met with the FOP and the chief of police. The two officers are claiming Aubrey's story is false. They are holding on to the fact they found her in the strip mall beaten. Even with the EMT's report, they aren't changing anything. Both officers are now on desk duty. Most likely, this will go to trial. The first step will be getting a grand jury to indict them. Once that happens, we'll go to trial and prove what they did…."

"Sorry to interrupt you. How many cases have you dealt with like this? What kind of attorney are you?" my dad inquired. I was surprised by the number of questions.

"I am a civil rights attorney. I have been working on cases like this since I was in law school interning," Pam answered my dad.

"How many cases have you won? How often did you get the public hyped up, the family excited, and nothing? How many cops were convicted? I don't care anything about a civil lawsuit. We don't need the money. I want justice."

My dad was on one today. Baby Maddox lay there sleeping, and my dad was on a roll.

"All of my cases don't involve cops. Some are between citizens. Others involve cops, employers, hospitals, and corporations. In some cases, I didn't win, but I have won 97% of my cases. I go after what my clients want me to go after. Some only want the money. Others want someone to be charged. I spoke to Tessa, and she wants me to go after both. They should be indicted, and she would like me to file a civil suit. Does that answer your questions?"

"Yes, it does."

"I have a question," I spoke up.

"Of course. Go ahead, Aubrey. I am here to serve you," Pam responded.

"Will I have to be on television? Will the media be involved?"

"Most likely, yes. We are fighting the police department, and they don't fight clean. I know it may make you uncomfortable, but we need the media on our side. We need to make this a nationwide case. I believe we have a good case. I have the pictures of you from the hospital. I have two different reports from the EMTs and the officers. I would have the video from the dashcam and their vest, but it was never turned on. I will request from the courts once we file the paperwork to grant me access to their tracker for that day. Each police car has a GPS on it. The tracker is saved in a database. So, we will know where they were. I want them fired, indicted, tried, found guilty, sentenced, and for the department to compensate you. It will not be easy, but I want you guys to trust me. This is my only case. I have given all of my other cases to my attorneys in my office."

"You own your firm?" I questioned.

"Yes, I do. I worked for the same law firm as an intern until three years after I passed my bar. I will be celebrating my 10th anniversary as a business owner in November. Do you have any other questions?"

"How will you work on the case if you live in Virginia?" I continued to ask.

"Good question. I have booked a suite here in Maryland. I will be staying here until the case is over."

"Girl, you could have stayed here with us. We have the room," my mother added. Why would she offer this lady a room in our house?

"No, that would not be a good idea. It would not be a good look if I stayed here."

"You don't have a family that will miss you," I inquired.

"I do. I have a husband and three kids. My husband owns an architecture firm, so he can work remotely if needed. But my mother-in-law will stay with him as long as we need her to," Pam politely told me.

"How old are your kids?" I asked because I wanted to know more.

"Aubrey, Pam's life has nothing to do with this case," my mother felt the need to add to the conversation.

"Tessa, it's okay. I'm glad Aubrey is inquiring about my life. I am about to get all into her life, so she deserves to know about mine. I have twin girls that are three, and my son is six. Do you have any other questions, Aubrey, Kevin, or Tessa?"

"I don't," I answered.

"I'm good," my dad added.

"What's next?" my mom asked.

"We kick ass and take down the police department."

Chapter 4: "Telling My Side"

"Hey Pamela, I know you told me to let you handle everything. But I couldn't just sit by and do nothing. We know the cops said they found Aubrey in the shopping center. There's a boutique on the end where they said she was found. I know the lady who owns the shop because I always buy clothes from them. This morning I was running errands, and I stopped by. I talked to the owner, LeAndra. She said she wasn't working that day, but her co-owner Free was. According to LeAndra, Free opened the store at 10:00 and didn't leave until 7:30. Another girl was also working. I don't know her name.

"LeAndra stated she would have Free call me when she comes in today. The big part is that the boutique has a camera inside and outside the store. There are two cameras—one point toward the parking lot and the other points toward the end of the shopping center. LeAndra let me look at it around the time everything happened, and there was no ambulance, police, or Aubrey. So, this is good, right?"

I overheard my mother talking to Pamela on the phone. She had her speakerphone on so I could hear the entire conversation. Finally, things might be turning around. It had been three weeks since we met Pamela and the police department was not budging. I'm supposed to get my wire and cast off this week. I go on Wednesday for my wire and Friday for the cast.

"This is great, Tessa. Do you think she'll allow us to use the video if needed? Did you tell her what happened to Aubrey?" Pamela responded.

"LeAndra told me I could use them if I needed. She wants Free to call me just in case we have any questions. I did tell her what had happened. With your advice, I told everyone what had happened. I have been posting Aubrey's pictures from when she was in the hospital on my social media pages. My family knows, and they have been very supportive. I am worried about what this is doing to Aubrey. She doesn't like her picture being blasted all over social media. As she would say, she's now a hashtag. This is a lot, and we haven't even gone in front of the media yet."

"I'm pretty sure we will need the video. I told you guys this was going to get serious. Our press conference tomorrow will bring even more attention. I am going to demand the officers be fired. It's been almost two months, and I am tired of their lies and them dragging their feet. Get ready. I told you last week that they will do everything they can to take your family down once we get in front of the media. They will dig into your past, Kevin's, his wife, Aubrey's life, and especially your marriage. Text me the boutique's number. I will call her if needed. I want you to step back from it. And I will see you tomorrow morning at 10:00 across the street from the police department. I have called all of my media contacts in Maryland and D.C. I'm sure they will all be there."

"Thanks. I'm going to talk to Aubrey, and I will see you tomorrow," my mother stated as she ended her call.

I was already standing outside my mom's office, so I figured I would speak up. "Ma, there's no need to talk to me about tomorrow. This is what we signed up for. I'm ready for whatever will come. Is daddy coming?"

"He told me he was. Your dad said he'll meet us here, and we'll ride together."

My mother's comment caught me off guard. "Why are we riding together? Are we supposed to be portraying a happy family?"

"No, that is not what we had planned. Pamela didn't think it would be a good look if we didn't arrive together. We are your parents, and we need to stick together. The last thing I want anyone trying to do is, portray your father as a dead-beat dad or me as a single mother. We're black, and the police department and the media will attempt to tear us apart. Your dad is a good father and provider. I'm not a single parent. Tomorrow, we will talk about the facts. After tomorrow, who knows what may happen."

***

I couldn't sleep at all that night. I could only think about being in front of a camera all day. What will it be like standing outside, across from the police station telling everyone what happened to me on that awful day? My mom went to sleep around 10:30. I know once her television is off, she's done for the night. I was so restless that I texted Jason, but he didn't respond. I started staring at the bookcase in my room. There were so many books I hadn't read yet. This one by Eric Jerome Dickey that my mom bought me years ago. I had been meaning to read it. Why didn't I read this book? What was it even about? Why did this one book stand out from all of the others? Should I start reading it now? These were all the questions that went through my mind that night. Of course, I never picked the book up. I lay in my bed staring at the ceiling. There were so many images appearing in my mind. It was my black eye. There was the image of my swollen lip. Then I saw my broken arm. My wires popped up. As soon as the images faded, I felt tears coming down my cheeks.

All night I was afraid. I knew I couldn't speak if anyone asked me a question. What was going to happen if Jason saw the news? I know he'll be mad because I lied to him. I wish I could have told him the truth, so I did. I sent Jason a text message at 1:29 am.

"Hey, Jason. I have been trying to reach you. You don't respond to my messages or calls. I know things have been crazy, lol. Sorry, not lol. This isn't funny. I'm just trying to laugh instead of crying. I want to tell you the truth before you see it on social media or on the news. I lied about being in a car accident. The police beat me up. It happened the day we were supposed to meet you at the mall. I was waiting for Allison in front of her house, and they pulled up. They started harassing me, and then it happened. I saw Allison standing there the whole time, watching from her window. I had a broken arm and jaw. Parts of my body were also bruised. My parents didn't want me to tell anyone, so I couldn't say anything. That's why I couldn't facetime you. I'm sorry. I hope you forgive me."

After I sent Jason a message, I went to sleep. I guess I needed to get that off my chest to sleep. My mother came into my room around 7:30 to wake me up. What's the point in having an alarm clock when you have a mother and curtains?

"Come on, Aubrey, it's time to get up. We need to leave here by 9:35," my mother stated.

"Why am I getting up this early? It's only going to take me an hour to get ready. I'm tired," I grumbled. I wanted her to get out of my room. I needed her to leave me alone.

"Aubrey, your dad will be here soon. I want you to eat before we leave."

"Okay fine," I screamed.

"Wait a minute. I know you have a lot going on, but you better not yell at me again."

"I'm sorry. Ma, I'm just tired, that's all."

"Get up," my mother demanded this time.

I put my covers over my face and rolled my eyes. I guess I didn't have a choice but to wake up. As I raised my body from my unbelievably comfortable mattress, I checked my phone. There was nothing from Jason. I can't believe he didn't respond. Jason is always up all night long. Now he doesn't want to respond. Oh well!

"Aubrey, baby, how are you feeling?"

"Grand-Grand, what are you doing here?"

"I told your mother I would attend the press conference with you guys. Some other family members will be there for support. You need all of the support you can get," Grand-Grand stated as she walked into my room.

I sighed because this was going to get out of hand. My mom's side of the family is huge. I know everyone will want to come here after the conference. My dad's side of the family is even bigger. I hope my mother tells everyone to go home.

"Okay. I'm going to take a shower."

"Can you eat solid food yet?" Grand-grand asked.

"Yes, ma'am."

"Do you want some breakfast? I can see what's in the kitchen and cook something. What do you want?"

"An omelet, soft bacon, and a croissant are fine," I responded.

"Do you want it as a sandwich?"

"No."

I went into my bathroom and ran my bath water. I usually shower, but I needed to soak on this day, plus my cast is still on until later this week. My mother gave me some bath bombs her assistant made. I tossed a bath bomb in the tub. The temperature was just right. I lay there for so long; my mother knocked on the door to see if I was okay.

"Aubrey, are you okay in there? Your food is getting cold."

"Oh, I will be out shortly."

When I went into my room, I checked my phone again. The only thing I saw was the clock reading 8:08. I still can't believe he hadn't responded. I really can't believe none of my friends hadn't reached out. I don't want to talk to Allison, but I have other friends. Why hadn't anyone asked me about not being in school? I know that bitch Allison probably said something. "Ugh," I screamed.

"Aubrey, Aubrey, are you okay?"

"Mom, I'm okay. Can I please have some time to myself? I'm trying to get my mind right."

"Fine," my mother stated in a frustrated tone.

I got dressed in the pantsuit my mother laid out for me. She wanted me to dress up to show some type of maturity. I'm a teenager. How mature should I be? I pulled my locs into a bun on top of my head and chose my diamond studs for jewelry. Today, my face will be filled with shea butter and nude lip gloss only. As I entered the kitchen to warm my food up, the first face I saw was my dad pouring a cup of coffee.

"Hey, I didn't think you would be here this early."

"Baby girl. How are you feeling?" my dad asked.

"I don't want to do this. I rather for all of this to disappear into thin air like my friends."

"Your friends? What happened?"

"Since I have been out of school, no one has contacted me. Jason stopped taking my calls. I don't know why," I cried.

"Aubrey, stop crying. Have you tried reaching out to any of your friends?"

"No!" I started to whine. Whenever I would whine, my dad would come to my defense.

"Not today. Your whining is not going to work in this situation. I don't know why your friends haven't contacted you. But things like this goes both ways. You can reach out to them also. Eat your breakfast so we can leave."

The ending to that conversation didn't go the way I wanted it to. I warmed my food up and started eating. As I finally was able to endure some peace this morning with a house filled with people, well, not filled, my mother was hyped up.

"All right, everyone, let's go. I want to get there on time. On-time means we're there early, not when it starts. Let's roll. Everyone meet me in the garage in 20 seconds."

"Tessa, calm your ass down. Dag," Grand-Grand demanded. I found it funny because my mother always wanted to take charge.

Even though Grand-Grand told her to calm down, everyone was in the garage, getting inside my mother's truck within 20 seconds. Because of her demand, I had to take my food with me. The drive to the police station was very quiet. My mother was playing a spiritual message from one of her favorite podcasts. My dad was texting Madison. I could tell it was her because of the smile on his face. Plus, I peeped his messages because he was sitting next to me. My grandmother was sitting up front with my mother, not saying anything. Me, I was scrolling through social media and nibbling on my food. I felt like I had become a stalker of my friend's pages. I haven't posted anything since everything happened. I left that to my mother. Before I could get into my feelings again about my friends, we pulled up to the designated spot.

I immediately saw Pamela standing up against a black Tesla, talking on the phone. There she was again in a sharp suit. Today she had a dark purple pair of slacks that fit her just right. She wore a black blouse and a pair of black patent leather pumps. Not too far from her were a bunch of news media trucks with reporters standing outside them. I'm assuming everyone was waiting to get started. My mom parked the truck, and we all went out simultaneously. It was like we planned to get out in a uniformed style. I placed my sunglasses on, knowing my mother would make me take them off when everything got started.

"Good morning, everyone. Are you guys ready to get started?" Pamela asked as we approached her.

"How long will this thing go on?" Grand-Grand questioned.

"Ma. Do you have somewhere to go? You didn't have to come," my mother answered before Pamela could.

"Tessa, what did I tell you back at the house? Calm down."

I could tell my mother wanted to roll her eyes, but she didn't dare. She stood there and didn't say anything. I was laughing on the inside.

"Ms. Janice, I am not sure how long it will take. I doubt if we're here for over an hour. It really will depend on how many questions everyone has. Aubrey, how are you feeling?"

"I'm good. I don't want to say anything, but I guess I'll have to."

"As we discussed, I did give the media pictures of Aubrey from the day she was in the hospital. When they play the story, the pictures will be aired. I know it will be a lot, but this is what we have to look forward to," Pamela explained to all of us. "Does anyone have any questions?"

We all shook our heads and headed towards the podium with Pamela in the lead. Pamela stood in front of the microphone while we all stood behind her. My mom insisted I move next to Pamela. I didn't want to, but I did it to appease her. I saw some of my family members standing off to the side. It wasn't as many as I thought. But it was a work day.

"Good morning, members of the media. I want to thank you all for coming out today. It is time for us to get started. On April 27, 2018, my client Aubrey Tucker was brutally assaulted by two police officers from the Walnut Grove district. A sixteen-year-old girl that barely weighs 140 pounds had her jaw and arm broken. Her body was badly bruised, and those two officers are still in uniform. Officer Lucy Cooper and Paul Brickley stopped Ms. Tucker while sitting outside her friend's house. Ms. Tucker was waiting for her friend to come out to go to the mall together. Instead, the officers pulled up, harassed, and then beat her. Not only did they do all of this, but they falsified their report. As all of this was going down, Captain Jennifer Black's daughter was standing in her window watching everything. Once Captain Black found out what happened, she covered everything up. She went directly to the hospital to intervene before Ms. Tessa Tucker arrived.

"I don't know why this event took place. The only thing I can think of is she's black. They saw a young black girl in a wealthy neighborhood and thought she didn't belong there. I am asking the Chief of Police to fire Officer Brickely, Officer Cooper, and Captain Black. I am also asking the district attorney to file charges against these officers. We have evidence they falsified paperwork; there was an attempt to cover up evidence; we have witnesses and a video that will help prove they didn't tell the truth in their report. In addition, they did not turn on their body or dashboard cam. I want to add one more thing: these officers were so close to Ms. Tucker that she could read their badge numbers as she was being beaten. Officer Cooper's badge number is 4836, and Officer Brickley's number is 4732. This shouldn't have happened, and I am demanding justice. Does anyone have any questions?"

"Mrs. Owens, can we hear from Aubrey?" a reporter in a white blazer asked.

"I will leave that up to Aubrey."

Pamela turned and looked at me. She nodded towards the podium as if she was asking if I wanted to speak but without her saying anything. I took a deep breath in, and as I walked toward the podium, my dad grabbed my hand and walked with me.

"I got you, baby girl," he whispered.

"Hi, what question do you have for me?" I questioned.

"What did you do for the officers to stop you?" the same reporter asked.

"I didn't do anything. I walked to my best friend's house like I do all the time. I sent her a text message letting her know I was outside. Instead of going in, I sat on the curb. This was something I always did. I knew Allison was on her way out. That's when the police car pulled up. I didn't do anything wrong," I answered. I was mad by the question, but Pamela told us ahead of time how they would spin it. She told each of us not to get upset.

"Mrs. Owens, will you be filing a civil suit?" a man reporter asked that was standing in the front. He was white and looked like he had on a hairpiece.

I stepped to the side and let Pamela answer that question. "I will not be answering that question at this moment. Any other questions?"

"Have you spoken to the Chief of Police?" a black woman reported asked. She had braids in her hair. I was happy to see a sister rocking braids as a news reporter.

"I have spoken to Chief Hoffman. I will not go into detail about our conversation, but he is willing to work with us."

"Why haven't they suspended the officers yet?" another black woman reporter asked. This lady had a natural twist out. I was smiling hard on the inside.

"I cannot answer that question. That is a question you would have to ask the chief. Does anyone else have any questions? I would like to get the Tuckers back home."

"Yes, what relationship does Captain Black have with the Tuckers?" a white reporter from the back asked.

"Captain Black's daughter and Aubrey attend the same school and are friends. Well, they were friends. Any other questions?"

There were so many questions coming through. Pamela answered questions for about 15 more minutes until it was time to go. As the reporters gathered their equipment and headed toward the truck, we noticed the group of police officers standing across the street from us. Pamela was right. She told us they would stand outside watching everything in anger. Pamela walked us to the truck and told us not to pay attention to them. When the media noticed they were watching, they ran toward them like hungry vultures.

"You did wonderful, Aubrey. I will be in touch tomorrow. I am pretty sure the FOP, the chief, and some lawyers will be contacting me within the next 24 hours. We just started a revolution, and things will get very heavy. But I am very confident justice will be served because of the evidence we have," Pamela confidently stated.

"Do you know how much evidence lawyers had in the past, and cops still got away with murder?" my dad angrily asked.

"I am aware, Mr. Tucker. Please be confident in me. If you guys have any other questions before tomorrow, don't hesitate to give me a call."

We all got into the truck and headed home.

"Ma, can we stop and grab some lunch?"

"Aubrey, we have food at home," my mom responded.

"I don't want the food at home. I want some cream of crab soup."

"I have a taste for some cream of crab soup also," Grand-Grand added.

"I don't feel like it or have time to stop. I need to run into the office for a meeting with my staff," my mom stated as she turned our request down.

"When we get back to the house, I'll get my car and go to the market. I can make the soup at the house," my dad offered.

"Thanks, dad."

* * *

Two hours later and something is happening that I never thought would. I am sitting at the dining room table eating cream of crab soup with my dad and grandmother.

They're eating fried catfish. I took a small piece but didn't want to do too much until my wire comes off. These two are talking about the orange man that's supposed to be running the country. There's no fighting or name-calling. I think I can get used to this. As I listened to them talk, I realized I never turned my phone back on. I turned it off once we arrived at the press conference. I don't know why I was worried about turning it back on because it's not like anyone called me. But I turned it on to a surprise. My worst nightmare is now a reality. #JusticeForAubreyTucker is a hashtag.

The press conference we did was blasted all over social media. They found every one of my social media pages and tagged me in posts. Since this morning, I searched for my new hashtag and found over one thousand posts. Then there were the text messages from everyone now.

"OMG, Aubrey. Call me," Kaley texted. Kaley is a freshman that's in the Black Student Union with me. We aren't friends. The only reason she has my number is because we all exchange numbers at the beginning of the school year.

"Aubrey, I always knew Allison was a snake. Call me," Sabrina texted. Sabrina was this white girl that thought she was black. I met her during our fifth-grade year. A black gay couple adopted her. Her biological parents were junkies, and she was placed in foster care at three. According to Sabrina, these two black men adopted her a year after she was in foster care. She loves her dads, but that girl believes she's black. You can't blame her since the only family she knows is black.

"Why did you lie on Allison? She told me everything you said was a lie. #Aubreyisaliar. By the way, it's Monica." Monica is not my friend. That's why she had to let me know who she was. Monica plays ice hockey with Allison. She's new to the school. This was her second year at Liberty Prep. Monica is an army brat. Her

dad had just retired from the army and moved to Maryland. Rumor is her mother is originally from Maryland, and she wanted to move closer to her parents. This girl that goes to our school named Bridgett is friends with Monica's cousin. Of course, she told Bridgett the dad cheated on her mother multiple times while in the military, and she was waiting for him to retire to leave. Either way, I don't know her well enough for her not to like me.

"We are going to stage a protest for you. Call me for the details. I am sorry this happened," Sapphire texted. Sapphire was also a member of the Black Student Union. She was the group's comedian but always came up with good ideas. Sapphire came to Liberty Prep during middle school. We were always friends, but we never got close as I did with Allison.

"Why didn't you call me? I asked Allison why you two didn't show up at the mall that day. She told us you were punished. I should have called you instead of asking her. I asked Jason why you weren't in school. He told me you were in a car accident. I guess you couldn't say anything. We are friends, why didn't you call me? Luv U," Bailey texted. Bailey was my right hand with BSU. She was my VP, and we played softball together. I know she should have been the one person I did call, but I didn't know what I could or couldn't say, like with Jason. I never said Bailey was my best friend, but we were close. I met Bailey in the second grade; she was my best friend then. Her family moved away in the middle of our fourth-grade year. Her mom is a Cardiologist. She was offered a job in Texas as the head of the Cardiology department at one of their top hospitals. They moved back here during our ninth-grade year when her grandfather got sick. When she walked into class that morning, I knew exactly who she was. I was surprised she remembered me, but I could never forget her. We became friends all over again.

"Yo, that bitch needs to be stomped. I can get my cousin from the city to jump her. Ha ha, I hope you're good. Call me," Zyair texted. He was the school basketball star, a member of BSU, and one of my friends. Zyair arrived at the school last year. He's only in the tenth, and the school offered him a full basketball scholarship. He is funny and always down for payback. That's what I like about him. He protects his friends. I don't know much about basketball, but they say all the top Division 1 schools are looking at him for a full scholarship.

There were so many text messages to go through, and I got tired of reading them. The one message I was looking for didn't come through. I wanted to hear from Jason, but he didn't want to hear from me. I got up from the table and left the two new best friends alone. I wanted to call Bailey to apologize for not telling her. I went into my room, closed the door, changed my clothes, and plopped down onto my bed.

"Alexa, turn on Solange's A Seat at the Table." Even though that album is old, it always puts me in a good mood.

"Girl, are you okay?" Bailey asked as she answered the phone on the second ring.

"Hey, I am okay physically. I'm sorry I didn't tell you," I responded.

"What in the hell happened? I should have called you, but Jason said you didn't want to talk to anyone."

"Bailey, don't worry about it. I couldn't tell anyone what had happened. Of course, I lied to Jason, but honestly, I didn't want to talk to anyone. But I was mad at all of you guys because no one called to see why I hadn't been in school," I confessed.

"I can't speak for anyone else, but I should have called you. When Jason told me you were in an accident, I didn't think it was that serious. He didn't say you were hurt or anything. But then, I started focusing on my finals, and you slipped my mind. Please forgive me," Bailey cried.

"Bailey, don't cry. It's okay. Even if you did call, I wouldn't have been able to tell you anything. It was a lot, and I don't want to relive that moment with you. I will have to talk about that day every time I'm in front of the media, a lawyer, in a courthouse, and probably for the rest of my life. With my friends, I want to talk about something else. I want you to know that I didn't do anything wrong. Allison stood there and watched those cops beat me and didn't do anything about it. I don't want to go through that day again with my friends. Do you understand?"

"Yes, I do, Aubrey. Can I ask you a question, though?"

"Yup."

"I saw your pictures from when you were in the hospital. Has everything healed completely?"

"My jaw and arm have healed. There is some pain at times if I do too much. There is a permanent mark on my back from the beating. I also have a scar on my cheek. I think when she hit me in the face, her ring cut me. I had three stitches in that spot. My cast and wires will be removed this week. Other than that, it's all mental. Any other questions?" I explained, trying to hold back my tears.

"I do have another question. When can we hang out? I can come to your house, or you can come over here. No one is here but my mom, brother, and grandma."

"Your brother?"

"Well, not my blood brother. He's my god-brother Sean. Sean moved in with us last year when his mom passed. She had a stroke. Sean dropped out of college, and you know my mom is pissed. She promised his mother that he would finish school."

"He dropped out of college. Why?" I screamed as if it was my brother.

"Technically, he didn't drop out. He told my mom he hated Virginia and wanted to attend college here in Maryland. Since he left school, studying abroad in London was canceled. So, he starts his junior year at a new school. For the summer, my mom got him a job at her hospital in the cafeteria."

"The cafeteria; why there?"

"His major is engineering, and if he had gone to London, they would have given him a paid internship. That didn't happen, so my mother told him he needed to make some money this summer. That was the fastest way for him to do it. Can you have company or come over?"

"My mom is at work, but I can ask her if it's okay for you to come over. My dad and grandmother are here. Everyone thinks I need a parent around all the time. I'm texting her now."

"While we're waiting for your mom to respond, what's up with you and Jason?"

"I don't know. You know I couldn't tell my parents about Jason. When I was finally able to work up the nerve to talk to him after everything happened, I couldn't talk. My mouth was still wired and in pain. The only thing I could do was text. I know I lied, but I had no other choice. I told my mother about him, and she flipped out because he was put out of his old school. I talked to my dad, and he came around. When I was ready to facetime him and confess. He wouldn't talk to me. I sent him a text message in the middle of the night about everything that happened. He was the first person I told. But nothing. I tried, but he ghosted me, and I stopped trying. I like Jason, but my daddy told me not to chase a man."

"I hear you, but I think it had a lot to do with Allison," Bailey added.

"Why would you say that?"

"Just before the school year ended, I started seeing those two hang out a lot. I figured it was because you were her best friend and Jason was your boyfriend. A couple of weeks after school was over, I went to the mall with my cousin, and I saw them in the food court together. I walked up to them and sat down. Jason said they ran into each other in Foot Locker. Allison was headed to the food court, and he was hungry too. So, I sat there with my cousin until one of them got up. Allison left after about 15 minutes of me sitting down. Once she left, I asked Jason what was up and if you two broke up. He said you two were taking a break and needed to confirm something with Allison. He was probably asking her if you got into a car accident since everything didn't come out until today."

"Do you think he knew I was lying about the car accident? Why would he think I was lying?" I questioned. This was very bizarre to me. As the conversation continued, my mom texted me and said it was okay for Bailey to come over.

"My mother said you can come over."

"Okay. I am going to get dressed and ask my mom. Then I'll be over. My mother lets me drive my grandma's car now that she can't drive anymore. Do you want me to bring you any food?"

"I will be glad when my mother lets me start driving school."

"Why haven't you gone to driving school yet. We're coming up on our senior year," Bailey shockingly asked.

"I am supposed to go this summer at the end of this month. I need to before this permit goes to waste. She did promise a car if I got my license."

"What kind of car are you going to get?"

"My mother said it had to be used, but it would be luxury. I would have settled for an Accord. You know she has an image to keep up with. How dare her daughter drive an average car? Most likely, it'll be a used Acura or Lexus."

"Okay. I will be over there soon. Do you want anything? I am going to get something to eat."

"No, and my dad cooked some fish and some cream of crab soup. It's a lot here."

"Ard. On my way," Bailey told me.

***

Bailey stayed at my house until around eight that night. It felt good to be around someone other than my mom. Bailey convinced me to get back on social media so people wouldn't think I was hiding. She had me making a bunch of videos of us dancing. I couldn't believe how silly we were acting, but I missed this. While we were together, more and more text messages came through asking how I was doing. There were some about the protest Sapphire was putting together. I received some hate DMs from Allison's family and some of her racist ass friends. Bailey told me to screenshot them just in case I needed them. She told me to tell my parents, but I sent them to Pamela. I'll let her deal with it. Today was long, but having Bailey around made things better. She told me to embrace being a hashtag. Bailey thinks something good will come out of this. I don't, but I love her optimism.

***

"Aubrey, how was your time with Bailey? I'm glad you finally got to see your friends," my mom stated as she barged into my room.

"We had fun. It felt good to put what happened back in April behind me."

"I'm sure you already know, but Pamela called me to let me know you have been trending."

My mother must have seen the look on my face. I knew I was hashtag but trending.

"Aubrey, I know this is the last thing you want, but this could be good on our end. Now that the country is becoming aware of everything that happened to you, we will have more people on our side. This is what we want. The police department is not going to fire them. The DA is not going to automatically charge them. We need to expose them, and since you are trending, this will help."

"Okay," I responded as I turned on my television. This was my signal for my mother to get out. Of course, she didn't take the hint.

"You can't respond with okay. I knew I shouldn't have let you stop going to therapy. I'm going to make an appointment in the morning."

"I can respond with okay, and I don't need therapy. I didn't like the first session, and I told you that. I know and understand what happened to me. There's no need for a stranger to keep bringing it up. I'm not going. Now can you leave me alone?"

"So, help me, god, if you ever in your life attempt to speak to me like that again, I will knock your ass across this room. I understand what you're going through, but the attitude needs to go. Clearly, the way you're reacting is the exact reason I said you're going back to therapy."

My mother walked out of my room and slammed the door without saying anything else. I already knew I was wrong once again for taking my anger out on her, but she got on my nerves. I wantedthe officers to be charged and convicted, but I didn't ask for the press conference. I didn't ask for a big-time lawyer. I didn't request to be isolated for over a month. And I didn't want to be a damn hashtag. Unless this happened to them, my mother and everyone else would never understand. I turned the television off and drowned myself in some music.

"Alexa, play me the best of my pop playlist," I whispered as I closed my eyes.

Barely opening my eyes, I turned over onto my left side and peeked at my phone. It was Jason calling me at 12:19 in the morning. I didn't even know I was asleep that long. "Alexa, stop playing my music."

"Hello," I answered in a groggy voice. I tried to clear my throat, but I still sounded like a man.

"Hi Aubrey, were you asleep?" Jason asked. His voice sounded so good. I missed talking to him.

"I fell asleep early, but I'm up now. What's up? Why are you calling me?" As bad as I wanted to talk to him, I couldn't let him know that.

"I'm not even going to lie. I know I haven't been in contact, but I was mad. I was mad with you because you kept beating around the bush about me seeing you. I was tired of you hiding me from your family as if I wasn't good enough. Then you send that text message about what happened. That made me even madder that you couldn't tell me the truth. First, I asked Allison about the car accident, and she told me you weren't in an accident. Then I asked Allison that morning after you sent the text about what you said, and she told me you were lying. It wasn't until I saw everything on social media and your pictures from the hospital. Then, I knew you were telling the truth. I was going to call earlier, but I was around my parents all day doing family things. My bad."

"Jason, if you had taken my calls, you would have known my dad said it was okay for me to date you. He wanted to meet you. Even though I wasn't completely healed and he wanted to meet you, I was ready to tell you the truth. The only reason I lied was because my mother said I couldn't tell anyone. She didn't even tell the school the truth about why I was out. I couldn't say anything. When you started ignoring me, I figured you were done. Then I found out you were hanging out with Allison."

"I know Bailey told you she saw me in the mall with Allison. I was only talking to her about what you told me about being in a car accident."

"Why wouldn't you believe me? I know I lied, but what made you question me about being in an accident? Why did you feel like you had to confirm my story again with the one person I told you was a part of this?" I yelled. I had never yelled at Jason before. We never even argued, but he was getting on my nerves.

"It wasn't that I didn't believe you...."

"It was exactly that. I told you what happened, and you had no reason to question it. You ghosted me because you didn't believe me. You had to see my face blasted all over the news before you would talk to me. What kind of boyfriend is that?"

"What kind of girlfriend would hide her boyfriend from her family as if she was ashamed of him?" Jason snapped back.

"I told you my parents wouldn't allow me to date. You chose to move forward," I snapped back.

"Aubrey, I didn't call you to argue. I apologize, but I'm not going to keep going back and forth with you. I'm sorry for what happened to you. I'm sorry for going behind your back and talking to Allison. Either you're going to forgive me or not. Which one?"

"Bye, Jason," I said before I hung up on him.

I wanted to talk to Jason for some time now, but he's not going to talk to me like he doesn't have any sense. He was my first boyfriend, but he definitely won't be my last. It's almost 1 am, and I am wide awake. What do I do? Go on social media. After Bailey left, I turned off all social media notifications. I only turned them on because of her. I don't know why but I have the urge to visit Allison's page. Everything hit me all over again. I WAS A FREAKING HASHTAG.

Chapter 5: "That's The Media for You"

"For them to prove their innocence, they will need a credible witness. It's Aubrey's word against a police department."

"A credible source told us that Captain Black's daughter didn't see anything. Allison, the daughter mentioned Aubrey never showed up at her house. Aubrey was always lying to her mother about where she was going. Aubrey was using Allison as a cover to sneak off with her boyfriend."

"Aubrey Tucker was not innocent. We don't know what happened but what if people listened to the police?"

"According to sources, Tessa Tucker has tried to settle behind closed doors. She's asking for an undisclosed amount, and if the county agrees, she will drop the charges. This makes you wonder if it was all about the money."

"No one knows too much about the dad. He stays out of the picture. Kevin Tucker appeared at one press conference. Was it a publicity stunt?"

"Students at Liberty Prep claims Aubrey Tucker was always talking about how much she hated the police."

Every station I turned to or social media outlet I was on, something negative was said about me. Since our first press conference, my family has done at least five more in person. I remember traveling to New York to appear on a major morning news outlet. We went to D.C for an appearance and so many others in Maryland. Some were in other states such as California, Texas, New Jersey, Florida, and Georgia. These were all virtual. This was my summer.

Everything was becoming overwhelming. It seemed like the more we defended ourselves, the more the media tried tearing me down. I didn't understand why I had to prove myself. The police are still claiming they found me in the shopping center. No one thought it would go on this long because LeAndra and Free were willing to give us the security footage from the day everything happened. Then someone broke into their store and destroyed their security equipment. Whoever did it didn't take any merchandise or money. LeAndra and Free were still willing to help us. They contacted the security company to get an online copy of the footage from the day of my incident and the break-in. To our surprise, the security company claimed they didn't have it. Coincidently, their systems were down on both days. Pamela later found out this particular company endorses the police department. She filed paperwork with the courts to demand the release of the footage. That could take weeks or months to receive.

I always watched these events when they happened to other people. I couldn't understand why no one believed them. Now, I am a living witness. It doesn't matter how much evidence you present; the police will never be wrong. In other news, my uncle is coming to town. My dad's brother Craig lives in Houston. My dad has a sister and brother. He's the oldest. My aunt Missy lives in Florida but doesn't speak to anyone in the family. She's still mad because no one likes her white racist and abusive husband. Everyone knew he was a racist and abuser from the start.

My dad planned to pick me up for dinner later. My uncle wanted to take me out to talk about everything. The only reason he wanted to talk is because he's a cop in Houston. I rarely hear from my uncle. I never hear from my cousins. He has two kids by two different women. My cousin, Rae, is a year older than me. I heard she's in hair school and didn't care for my uncle because he didn't buy her a car for graduation—dumb, right. Rae was always spoiled. I guess she was so used to getting what she wanted. My uncle hasn't spoken to Rae in a year, and I guess that's why she stopped talking to me.

My younger cousin, Ryan, is 14. Ryan lives here in Maryland. My uncle has been living in Texas for over 20 years. He moved there a few years after graduating high school for college. He dropped out during his sophomore year and joined the police force. He came home for vacation one year, hooked up with someone he went to high school with and returned to Texas. Later, we all found out she was pregnant. My uncle takes care of his kids financially but doesn't spend much time with them. Well, he did with Rae until she got mad at him. Ryan's mom moved them to the Eastern Shore, so we don't see him as much.

I said all that to say; that he needs to focus on being around his kids and not trying to preach to me about my thoughts on the police. Because I love my dad and haven't seen him in two weeks, I agreed to have dinner with them.

"Aubrey, your dad is here," my mom screamed from the bottom of the stairs.

I stared at my Pink slides trying to decide which ones I should wear. This was always a hard decision during the summer. I chose my black and white ones, grabbed my fanny pack, and went to see my father. My mother doesn't like my uncle. When I came downstairs, she was in her office with the door closed.

"Hey, daddy and Uncle Craig. Ma, I'm leaving."

"Okay, enjoy," my mom rebutted from her office.

"Tessa," my dad and uncle said in unison.

"Kevin, I will see you two when you get back." My mother is so petty.

"I see she still doesn't like me," my uncle tried to whisper.

"If you know that, why are you in my house?" my mother responded. Before my uncle could respond, my dad pushed him out of the house.

We drove to a restaurant not too far from my house. The car ride consisted of my uncle talking about his promotion and how much money he's making now. He went on and on about this four-bedroom, three-bath house with a two-car garage he was in the process of buying. Why does a single man need such a big house?

"So, Aubrey, what colleges are you looking at? What's your major?" my uncle quizzed.

"My major will be education, and I am looking at Bowie, Hampton, Spelman, Howard, and North Carolina Central are my top five."

"Why all HBCUs? I never understood the hype around HBCUs."

"You wouldn't understand because you didn't attend one. There's nothing wrong with my top five being HBCUs."

"What other choices are you looking at?"

"There are a lot of other ones. So, why did you want to see me? I know it's not about college. What about the police do you want to talk about?" I grilled.

"Man, you got a straight shooter here. First, Aubrey, I want to say I'm sorry for what happened to you. I wasn't there, so I don't know what took place…."

"Where are you going with this?"

"Hear me out, Aubrey. We all know there are some good cops and some bad cops. But I don't see why a cop would beat a teenage girl as you claimed. Do you remember what took place that day? Did you have a head injury?"

I could tell my dad was fuming, but I stepped in before he could say anything. "Let me explain something to you, Uncle Tom, sorry Craig. I don't care anything about good or bad cops. I know exactly what happened to me on that day. I remember being harassed because they thought this nappy-headed black girl didn't belong in such a wealthy neighborhood. I can recall watching my so-called best friend standing in the window as I was hit over and over again. I remember being unable to talk or move how and when I wanted to. To answer your question, I remember everything that happened which will haunt me for the rest of my life. I don't care what you do for a living, but I expected you, as my uncle, to have my back."

The table was silent until I started talking again.

"Can I order my tacos to go if there are no more questions about what I do and don't remember? I will rather be home with my mother. I want to be around someone that cares about me and doesn't question anything I say."

"Craig, you are out of line. Aubrey doesn't have a reason to lie," my dad said, but his response was garbage.

"Everyone relax. I was only trying to prepare you for what's to come," my uncle lied. He was trying to cover his tracks.

"I have already experienced 'what's to come,' uncle. I'm not trying to disrespect you, but I need you to stop talking. Daddy, please take me home."

"Aubrey, you haven't even ordered your food," my uncle added.

"Daddy, take me home, or I will call mom and ask her to come and get me."

That was the end of our meal. My dad took me back home and left with my uncle. He promised to call me after dropping my uncle off at his hotel. I couldn't believe the words that came out of his mouth. I already know my mother will want to know why I returned so soon. I figured I would tell her before she asks.

"Hey Ma, can we talk?"

"Yeah, why are you back so early?" she questioned.

"That's what I wanted to talk about. Uncle Craig started questioning me about what happened that day. He had the nerve to ask me if I remembered what occurred. Then he tried to play the good cop bad cop card. Ma, I was trying not to disrespect him, but I never expected to hear any of it from family. I have heard it from the media daily, but my uncle. Daddy's side of the family is messed up for real."

"I can't believe that bastard would do that. What did your father say?"

"Nothing much. I asked him to bring me home. Are you cooking dinner?"

"I didn't plan to Aubrey because you were going out. Do you want to order something?"

"Yeah, and it doesn't matter what. I'm going upstairs to call Bailey," I told my mom.

"Don't forget you are going back to therapy tomorrow. I don't want to hear back talk about it either," my mom demanded.

"I didn't forget. Ma, I have a question, and don't lie."

"What?"

"Are you still talking to Dr. Chambers?" I asked, waiting for her to lie.

"Why would you ask me something like that? Who told you I was talking to Dr. Chambers?" my mom stuttered as she started questioning me.

"Ma, I know you have been talking to him on the phone. The question is, have you two gone on a date yet? I think it's best if you finally start dating again. And Dr. Chambers is a catch."

"Okay, you got me. We went out one time, but our schedules kept clashing. We talked on the phone, but he suggested scaling back because of the lawsuit. He doesn't want the media or anyone else bringing him up, which may hurt our case. They could say he's lying about your injuries because we're dating. I agree with him. For now, the phone is what it is. I want to talk to you about something else," my mom explained.

"What's wrong?"

"A while ago, Pamela presented their lawyers with the paperwork from the EMTs. The EMT's paperwork is different from what the officers wrote up. We already knew that. Now they are saying one of the EMTs was fired because they found out he falsified paperwork in the past. The other EMT still has her job. They claim she went along with her partner because he had seniority."

"What does all of that mean?" I inquired.

"It means they are doing everything in their power to have this case dismissed. We are going to keep fighting. What reason would he have to falsify paperwork? The officers lied."

"So, someone stole the security footage from the store, and now this. Let's just drop everything so I can return to my normal life," I added before heading upstairs.

I knew my mom wasn't going to follow me upstairs. I think she has learned by now that when I want to be alone, it's best to leave me alone. All of this was straight-up bullshit. I needed to call Bailey because she will give me the rundown on the protest. I already told her I'm not attending because I have therapy, but I still want to know the plan.

"Hey Aubrey, I thought you were calling later," Bailey stated after two rings.

"I was, but my dinner was canceled. What are the details for tomorrow?"

"We plan to start the protest at the school and march to the police department. That's about a 10-mile walk. Sabrina made most of the signs, and her dads will make sure we have water. Sapphire and Zyair passed out the flyers, and we're expecting over 100 people. Zyair's aunt has a hookup with the county. So, they will close off the streets we need to march. And the police cannot stop our protest. We plan to chant once we arrive at the station until we're ready to leave. We are going to protest every day until you get justice. We're going to fight for you, sis."

"Thank you, guys, so much."

"How are you feeling, though?" Bailey asked in her motherly voice.

"I'm good. I guess. I don't want to go to therapy tomorrow. I feel like it's a waste of my time. I don't want to express my feelings. It doesn't matter how many people I tell; none of this is going away. My mother is forcing me to go. My dad thinks I should go, but he said it's up to me."

"Damn, that's messed up. Why don't you tell your mother you're not ready to talk about it?" Bailey suggested.

"I have been telling her that. My mother thinks she knows everything. In her mind, she's the only person that knows what's best for me."

"Did you tell her the protest was tomorrow? Why don't you tell her you want to go, and you'll go to therapy another day?"

"There are a lot of reasons why none of that will work. My lawyer doesn't think it's a good idea for me to be at the protest. She's afraid the police will target me and try to provoke me to do something. If they do that, I will lose my case. Plus, I rescheduled therapy about three times already," I explained.

"Just say you're sick and having flashbacks."

"If I tell her I'm having flashbacks, she will make me go. I could tell her my jaw was starting to hurt again. The worst thing she can do is make me a doctor's appointment. I think that might work. I'm going to tell her now and text you later."

After getting off the phone with Bailey, I sat in my room for about an hour. I hated lying to my mother, but therapy is not my thing. I know therapy is important and needed, but I'm wasn't ready. I hate that she was trying to force me to be ready. I wanted to talk about it, but I didn't want someone trying to fix me. I'm not broken. Yeah, my body parts were broken, but I'm not. I don't need to sit in front of someone once a week and talk about my life. I'll be 17 on August 29th, which is coming up pretty soon. This is not how I pictured it.

I remember when my parents planned my sweet sixteen, I was ecstatic. My parents rented out this hall that holds 300 people in Laurel. Everyone from my family was there. All of my friends and some classmates that aren't necessarily my friends were there. I remember that night like it was yesterday. I wore a custom red sequin dress and a pair of black Louis Vuitton pumps. My dreads were touched up that morning and placed in an up style. My makeup was on point with a natural look. Happy birthday was highlighted throughout the hall, on the walls, ceiling, and floor all night. The DJ made sure of that.

The food was all of my favorites. My dad wanted to cook, but I told him he shouldn't have to cook for my birthday, but he insisted. He pulled his team together and delivered a feast everyone had talked about for days. The appetizers were crab balls, buffalo chicken dip with pieces of French bread, fried crab sticks, nachos with cheese, macaroni bites, and buffalo wings. There were three types of salads to choose from. We had a garden salad, Greek salad, and Caesar salad. My guest had an option to choose from fried chicken, baked chicken, salmon, beef ribs, stuffed shrimp, and fried catfish. To go with the different types of meat and fish, we offered macaroni and cheese, string beans, mixed vegetables, loaded baked potatoes, greens, and red roasted potatoes. And finally, my favorite dish, my dad personally made alfredo with shrimp, chicken, crabmeat, and lobster. There was an assortment of different flavored cupcakes. My mom's receptionist made a two-tiered carrot cake with cream cheese icing.

I remember my mother asking me if I wanted her to put a plate to the side, and I told her no. I figured there would be food left at the end, but there was nothing. But my father was always on point because he made me my own alfredo that he left at the house. The hall was set up as if someone was getting married. The colors were red, black, and silver. The tables were draped in red table cloth and silver centerpieces on each table. I had a red carpet, and the DJ played one of my favorite songs when I walked in. My mom was on my right side, and my dad was on the left as I walked in. They escorted me in as if I was a queen. Everyone was standing up in silence. No one said anything. I made sure the DJ instructed them to be quiet because I needed to hear the full song.

My table was set up with a chair fit for a queen—the party planner decorated it with red and silver everything. My chair was silver, and I had a personalized backdrop behind me. I wanted that so that when the photographer took pictures of me at the table, she wouldn't get the wall. My parents sat at the table with me also. There was one table for gifts in the corner, but they added two more. There were so many gifts, and my mom refused to have any placed on the floor.

When I mailed out the invitations, I told everyone to be there by 8:15 because we had a special surprise. If they were late, they would miss it. The surprise was me making my grand entrance. I know that may seem shallow, but I wanted everyone to see me walk in. I walked in at 8:30, and we partied until 1 in the morning. I was on such a natural high that I didn't go to sleep until 4:00. During my party, there was a part where my guest was allowed to come to the mic and say something special about me. I think everyone went up there, even my ugly stepmother. Besides my parent's speech, my most memorable one was Allison's. She had so many good things to say about me. I cried and had to go into the back room to get my makeup touched up.

Allison was my best friend. As I think about everything that happened, I can't believe she hadn't told the truth. How do you claim to be someone's sister? Not their best friend but sis and turn around and lie to protect some white assholes in blue. I hate her for all of this. Allison could have walked out of her house and stopped everything. She could have told the police I was waiting for her. My jaw and arm wouldn't have been broken if Allison had told them who her mother was.

"No more tears Aubrey. What happened, happened. Allison let you know who she stood with," I boldly told myself before I went to speak to my mom.

"Hey, mom, did the food get here yet?"

"The app says they are on the way. You good?"

"Yes and no," I answered as I got ready to tell my lie.

"What's wrong, Aubrey? Are you still mad about your uncle?"

I shook my head no. I was trying to play the role of my jaw hurting—less talking and more sad face.

"What's going on?"

"My jaw is starting to hurt. Can I skip therapy tomorrow? I feel like if I sit there and talk for hours, it'll hurt even more," I mumbled.

"Well, you're not going to be there for hours. It's 45 minutes, and you have canceled too many times already."

It was time to bring on the tears. There are a few things that can make me cry on the spot. My dad being with Madison and picturing Allison standing in the window watching me. Just like that, the tears started rolling. "Ma, please, it hurts bad."

"I'm canceling it. I will call your doctor on Monday to see if I can get you an appointment. If they charge me a fee for canceling, it's coming out of your pocket."

I shook my head yes and headed back towards my bedroom. I wanted to smirk, but I couldn't.

"Oh, Aubrey, how are you going to eat your food? I ordered tacos."

"Did you get the soft or hard tacos?" I questioned.

"I got three soft tacos with shrimp and a salad."

"I will try to eat the tacos tomorrow. I'm sure I can eat the salad."

"Okay, don't force it. Fix a smoothie if you think it will make it worse."

"Let me know when the food comes. I'm going to use the bathroom," I lied again. I didn't need to use the bathroom. I wanted to get away from her.

***

I woke up the next morning feeling overwhelmed. I had a sense that something bad would happen at that protest. I looked at my phone, and the protest was starting in 20 minutes. I called Bailey, but she didn't answer. I called Zyair, but he didn't answer. Finally, I walked into my bathroom, took a shower, and brushed my teeth. I know my mom is going to ask me about my mouth. I plan to stay in my room until she comes to me.

By the time I put some clothes on, the protest had started. It was live on social media, and almost every media coverage was airing it. They are showing several protests in different states. Bailey didn't tell me it was going to be like this. I thought the protest was only here in my county.

"Maaaaaaa," I screamed.

"Aubrey, what's wrong?" my mother asked, sounding out of breath.

"Look at the television. The protest about me is taken place in multiple states. Look at this."

"Aubrey, did you know about this?"

"No, Bailey told me about the one they planned here. Hold up, have you been downstairs yet?"

"No, I was lying in my room reading when you called. I haven't left out of my room since I woke up. Why?"

"Listen. Do you hear that noise? Do you hear people talking?"

My mother and I ran to my bedroom window, and the media were camped outside of our house. They were set up in front of our driveway. I guess they were waiting for someone to come out.

"Aubrey, call your dad and tell him to get here now. I'm going to get dressed and have them leave."

My mother put on some sweatpants and a t-shirt and made her way downstairs. After telling my dad what was going on, I followed my mother. She went to the alarm keypad and turned the alarm off. I was on her heels like a toddler following their mother to the bathroom. We went to the garage to request for them to leave. Just before my mother opened the garage door, she called Pamela.

"Pamela, I'm sorry for calling you this morning, but we have a problem."

"I have been looking at the news. I didn't know it was going to be this big. But this is a good thing. There are so many people on Aubrey's side," Pamela stated through the speakerphone.

"Yeah, yeah, that's fine. That's not my issue. We woke up to the media standing outside of my house. How did they get my address? What should I do? I don't want them here," my mother hysterically yelled through the phone. I could tell she was upset because her eyes were turning red. I could also tell she was trying to hold back her tears.

"Pamela, I want justice, but I don't want them invading our space. My damn daughter is here. They don't need to be harassing her."

"I can't get to you right now. I drove home last night for my daughter's birthday party this afternoon. Don't worry; I will be back Sunday night. Get yourself together, wipe the tears from your eyes and politely ask them to leave. Remind them this is private property, and if they don't leave, you will call the police."

"Really, what the hell is the police going to do? They might not show up."

"I know, but unless you want to give a statement which I don't recommend, this is what's best."

"Okay."

"Tessa, call me if you need me."

My mother stood tall, wiped her face, and, forgetting to put on her slides, she opened the garage door and walked outside barefoot. I was afraid to go beyond the garage door, but I could hear everything.

"Ma'am could you offer a statement about the protest for your daughter?" a white lady reporter asked. She looked like a barbie doll that had a lot of plastic surgery.

"Excuse me, can your daughter let us know her thoughts about the protest?" a black lady yelled out. I saw this reporter on the news before. She is a Karen in my eyes. Every time something happens to a black person, she finds a reason to bring up something about their past. She's always blaming the victim. I don't like her.

"Why isn't Aubrey at the protest? The protest is for her," a young white reporter asked. Even though I'm not into white men, he is cute.

"Excuse me. This is private property. I am requesting that you leave," my mother said.

"We can step into the street, which is not private property. We have a legal right to be here," the black lady reporter added. She's getting on my nerves.

"Please respect our privacy. If there is anything you would like to know, you can reach out to our attorney."

As my mother was walking away, my dad pulled up. How did he get here so fast? He honked his horn and demanded the media to move out of the driveway. This was the one time my mom didn't mind him parking there.

"Dad, how did you get here so fast?" I asked. I was talking to myself because he couldn't hear me.

My dad walked toward my mom and escorted her back to the garage. When he reached me, he hugged me and closed the garage door.

"How did you get here so fast?" I asked again.

"I was on the way from the airport. I dropped Craig off. He decided to leave earlier than planned. What is going on?"

"There are protest around the country about Aubrey. We looked outside, and they were there. Pamela told me to ask them to leave, but they won't leave. This is so embarrassing. Look at my neighbors watching this."

"Ma, are you serious? You're worried about what these people will think?" I yelled as I stormed back into the house.

"Tessa, you know damn well that comment was wrong."

"Kevin, I didn't mean it like that. I just don't want all of this attention around my house. I don't need anyone talking about us. This is embarrassing. That's the truth."

"I don't care what these people think," I yelled back into the garage.

My parents came into the house, forgetting about the news being outside.

"Aubrey, I am sorry for saying that. I don't want them talking to our neighbors. Even though we get along with everyone, you never know what someone might say. That's all I meant."

"Well, it's too late because they are talking to Mrs. Joan from across the street," I pointed out.

"Of course, her nosey ass would be the first person to come outside. We never did anything to her, so; I'm not worried."

"What do you need me to do, Tessa? I can stay for a while, but Madison and I had plans to spend time with Maddox today."

"Are you serious right now, Kevin? Your daughter is going through something, and you're worried about spending time with your wife," my mother rebutted.

"Tessa, you know damn well I love my daughter, but I have a son also. I have been neglecting my son because I have been giving Aubrey a lot of attention. I want to be here for Aubrey, but I need to be there for my other child. I'm not blowing her off. I have a right to split my time between both kids."

"I guess you wouldn't have this problem if you didn't cheat on me. If you had kept your thing between your legs, maybe none of this would have happened. Be a man and admit you messed up. You can leave, bye. We have been doing this without you for a long time."

"Doing what, Tessa? You act like I don't take care of my daughter. I take care of her financially, and I spend time with her. I am the same father I was when I was living here. I need you to get over us being over. I messed up, but it's done. We are not an item anymore, and I don't have to explain anything to you. I only owe Aubrey an explanation. This conversation is over," my dad screamed before turning to me. I looked into his eyes, and I could see he was hurting. He held his tears like my mom, but his eyes were red.

"Dad, thank you for coming over so fast. I understand you have to spend time with Maddox also. I'm okay," I assured my dad.

"Thank you for understanding. Do you need anything from me before I leave?"

"I wish you could make them leave, but I don't want you to get into trouble. Go ahead and spend time with Maddox. I'm going upstairs to watch the protest. They'll leave soon, hopefully. I love you, daddy."

"I love you too, sweetheart. Call me later."

Without saying anything to my mom, he walked out the front door and drove away. I will always understand why my mother is mad, but she needs to let it go. My dad is not coming back. I wish she would get a boyfriend so she could stop blaming my father for everything.

"Aubrey, why didn't you say how you felt? You should have told him you needed him to stay. Start standing up for yourself," my mom accused.

"What? What do you mean? I told him exactly how I felt. You have a problem with him, not me. Yes, I get upset when I think about him cheating, but he is a good father. That issue is between you and him, not me. He has a right to split his time between both kids. I'm not his only child. I will never make him feel bad for wanting to be a good father to his son. Maybe if you found your own man, you wouldn't worry about what he's doing."

"Excuse me, young lady."

"Oh, and by the way, I stand up for myself. The last time I stood up for myself, I was beaten." I yelled as I walked to my room. "How did this become about me? You have a yard full of news reporters, and you're mad at dad and me," I added as I stopped in the middle of the stairs.

I went into my room and slammed the door. I want her to get over my dad and move on. She projects her anger on everyone, and it's beyond annoying. As I sat on my bed to watch the protest, I heard my mother coming up the stairs, then her bedroom door closed. I turned on my television and pulled it up on my phone through social media. Every news channel was talking about the protest, even the big networks. The police were posted up at each location. As I switched back and forth between channels, some locations got out of hand. There were a lot of arrests, people hurt, looting, and then tear gas was thrown by police in DC because they got close to the capital.

I needed Bailey or one of my friends to call me. I was worried about all of them. I guess they couldn't talk to me since they were marching on my behalf. I turned my eyes to the news just in time for a picture of Jason and me being blasted across the screen.

"One of our sources sent us this picture of Aubrey Tucker and her boyfriend, Jason Weber. From what we are told, Jason is not a great influence on Aubrey. He was expelled from his previous school for drug possession. Is it possible she was in the area trying to sell drugs?" the white male anchor stated.

"Well, John, that is possible. If her boyfriend is a drug dealer, why would he get her to do his dirty work? They find a young girl from an upscale neighborhood and get her to sell their drugs," the white, redhead woman responded.

"Why would she try to sell drugs in front of a police captain's house?" the male anchor continued to question.

"John, as I think about it, maybe she was there trying to rob a house. If her boyfriend is a drug user or dealer, Aubrey Tucker could have been there trying to rob someone to feed their drug habit," the woman anchor added.

"You may be right, Amber. But, hold on, we're getting breaking news from the capital."

The news was now tuned into what was going on in DC. They were now showing a group of black protestors lined up against the wall handcuffed. They were being arrested because of me. I needed to see what was going on here in my area. I checked my local news, and they were talking about DC also. I looked back at social media and saw Bailey was live from her page. It looked like everything was peaceful.

A Week Later

"Tessa and Aubrey, will Kevin be joining us?" Pamela questioned.

My mother and I were sitting inside Pamela's hotel room. We were on our way to another interview. As always, she wanted to prepare us before we arrived. Pamela always wanted my dad at the interviews to show a united front. But, since my parents' last argument, my dad hasn't been over. I have talked to him on the phone, but that's it.

107

I love my dad because he always tells me how he feels. When we spoke the next day, my dad confessed that he would not come around as much. He's tired of my mom always throwing his mistakes up in his face every chance she gets. I hate to think my mother is bitter, but that is how she comes across. I get tired of hearing them argue and mainly hear her throwing shots. My mother doesn't know, but my dad is not coming.

"Daddy is not coming," I blurted out.

"What? Why? How do you know? When was the last time you spoke to him?" my mother went on and on.

"I talked to him last night. He couldn't take off today. They have a big catering event he needs to attend," I lied.

"Typical him," my mother stated as she rolled her eyes. "What do we do now?"

"Tessa, this is not an issue. We can interview without him." Pamela explained.

"Hell no. We need to be together. Everyone needs to see us as a family. If he doesn't show up, it looks bad."

"Tessa, trust me, it's okay. I'll smooth it over if they ask by redirecting the question to something else. Let's get ready to go so we won't be late."

***

"Mrs. Owens, thank you for coming in today and bringing your clients."

"Rachel, thank you for having us. This is Tessa Tucker and her daughter Aubrey Tucker," Pamela introduced us.

"Will Mr. Tucker be joining us?" Rachel asked.

"No, he had an emergency at work. Being a successful chef, sometimes duty calls. You know how that goes. When the news is hot, you have to drop everything. Right Rachel?" Pamela answered.

"Yes, I do. If you three would follow me. My producer will set you guys up with your mics and some water. I will be back in about five minutes, and we can get started."

There was something about this lady that I didn't like. She didn't seem trustworthy, but Pamela told us she's a good reporter. My instinct was right. Good ole Rachel did everything in her power to tear us down.

"Welcome back, everyone. Today I'm talking to Attorney Pamela Owens and her clients, Tessa and Aubrey Tucker. Unless you have been under a rock, you know about the alleged assault on Aubrey Tucker. Aubrey, can you take us through that day this incident was supposed to have occurred?"

"Aubrey, before you answer, Rachel, let's not use the words allege or supposed. This incident did occur between Aubrey and the police. There is no evidence that someone else beat her," Pamela interrupted.

"There's also no evidence the police did this," Rachel retorted.

"The reason there's no evidence is that the cops turned their dashcam and bodycam off. They are supposed to have both on when they leave the station. No one can explain that, can they?" Pamela spit.

"Okay, if you say so. Aubrey, can you tell us what happened that day?" Rachel asked again.

"I walked to my best friend, former best friend's house like I always do. I sent her a text letting her know I was outside when I arrived. I felt like there was no need for me to go in. She,

Allison, told me she was coming out. I sat on the curb, and the cops pulled up. They started asking me questions, and I answered each one. The male cop was the aggressor. He was encouraging the female cop to harass me. I tried to explain over and over again why I was there. I knew what to do in this situation. I put my hands up and kept them in the air.

"I asked them if I could get my ID and was told no. The female cop snatched my purse off my shoulders and dumped everything on the ground. She found my school ID and questioned me about where I lived. I asked if I could call my mother, and they told me no. The male cop then mentioned something about letting me get away with what was going on. The next thing I knew, I was punched in the face and kicked over and over again. The entire time Allison stood in the window watching…."

"Aubrey, before you go on. How do you know Allison saw everything if you were on the ground? How could you see her?" Rachel asked. She was sneaky.

"Like most houses around there, Allison's driveway is on a slant. I was at the bottom of the driveway. I faced her living room window when I started walking away from the cops. That is when I saw her staring at me. I did turn around when I was told to stop. When she hit me, I fell to the ground and looked up at the window. I needed help, and Allison saw me. She looked me in my eyes. I knew I was on my own at that point. I was placed in handcuffs and put in the back of the car. From there, I was beaten more and ended up in the hospital with a broken arm and jaw, along with some bruising," I continued to explain.

"Aubrey, I would like to say I am sorry this happened to you and whoever did this need to pay. Thank you for sharing your story with us. Can you tell us about Jason?"

"No, Aubrey will not answer that question," Pamela interrupted.

"Mrs. Owens, we only want to know about Jason and his role in everything."

"Rachel, you and every other news outlet should be ashamed of yourself. You are tarnishing this young man's name and putting him in something that has nothing to do with him. He has nothing to do with what happened to Aubrey. I am not going to allow you to tear down another black teenager," Pamela spoke up.

"Mrs. Owens, I am not trying to get you upset. I would like to clear up things. The police said Aubrey was in the area trying to sell or buy drugs. We're aware that this Jason fellow was kicked out of school for drug possession…."

"Do you know what a micro assault is? Before you can lie and say you do, I'm going to tell you. It is when you misuse your power and privilege in subtle ways to marginalize someone and create a different outcome based on their race. This is what you are doing, Rachel. You are using your white privilege to disgrace his name and create your own outcome on what you believe happened. If Aubrey or this young man were white, we wouldn't be having this conversation," Pamela continued to spat.

"Please…"

"This interview is over. Rachel, I came here so Aubrey could tell her story. You have done nothing but try to prove she's not the victim. Everything is alleged or supposed to, and I'm not okay with it. Jason does not have anything to do with this. I don't know what may or may not have happened to him. I do know Aubrey doesn't do or sell drugs. And I am 100% sure Jason doesn't either. Aubrey and Tessa, remove your mics, and let's go."

"Are you going to end the interview like that?" Rachel questioned with a stunned look on her face.

"Oh, yes, I am. This interview is over."

"I haven't had a chance to speak with Mrs. Tucker or to ask about Mr. Tucker," Rachel added.

"And you will not have a chance to do either. Have a nice day."

From that last sentence, our mics came off, I heard someone say go to commercial, and we walked out of the studio. Once we walked into the hallway, one of the producers came running out to talk to us. They sent the black guy out.

"Excuse me. Please don't leave yet. Rachel, sorry, Mrs. Halstead apologizes if she made you uncomfortable. She would like for you to come back and continue the interview."

"I'm sorry, Brother. Yeah, I called you brother because they sent the only black producer out here to try and smooth things over. You saw what she did in there. How dare you be okay with asking us to come back?" Pamela yelled. I had never seen her respond like this before. She has always been professional.

"My name is Shane. I'm not the enemy, ma'am. I am here to do my job, and that's it. I have nothing to do with the questions she asked. I think it's important for Aubrey to tell her story."

"Shane, no, thank you. We are leaving. Aubrey has told her story over and over again. Right now, it's time for her to stop telling her story. It's time for those cops to be arrested. Have a great day."

After Pamela's final remark, we walked out of the studio and drove back to her hotel to get my mom's truck. Everyone was quiet during the ride. The only thing Pamela said once we arrived at the hotel's parking lot was, "That's the media for you. I will call you later today with any updates."

Chapter 6: "Threats and Security"

A couple of weeks had passed by after our last in-person interview. Pamela stopped taking interview requests because she was tired of me being attacked. After the interview, things didn't get any better. There was more protest all over the country, and most of them turned violent. My mom is losing her mind because my dad will not return her calls. He's only talking to me. I keep telling her to stop fussing with him, but she doesn't see that she's doing anything wrong. I haven't seen my father other than on facetime because of their bickering. Outside of those two, everything has been good. I finished driving school, and since I already had my driving hours, I can take my test soon.

"Ma, are we still going to look at cars today?"

"Aubrey, you haven't even taken your test yet. What's the rush?" my mom questioned. I hated when she did that. She'll say one thing and then change her mind.

"You know I can drive. Last week, you promised that we could look at cars today. Why did you change your mind?"

"I didn't change my mind. I don't understand the rush. We can still go."

"Thank you," I stated before she could say anything else.

Just as I was about to fix myself a bowl of butter pecan ice cream with caramel, the doorbell rang. I walked to the window and peeped out to see who was there. I was shocked by the person that was boldly standing on my porch.

"Ma, I think you should get the door."

"Aubrey, who is it? Is it someone from the news? They are getting on my nerves," my mother questioned.

My mother didn't even look out the peephole; I wish she did.

"What the hell are you doing on my porch David?"

David is Jennifer's husband. My mother can't stand David because she knows he doesn't like black women. He's black; from my understanding, he never dated a black woman. Jennifer told my mom his issue is not with all black women but his mother. His mother gave him up for adoption because he was a product of rape. She was raped as a teenager. A white family adopted him. A family full of cops, which is how he became a state trooper.

Allison told me he met his birth mother when he was a teenager. He went looking and found her. She agreed to speak with him but cut the meeting short because he cussed her out. David didn't understand her reasoning behind giving him up for adoption, especially since she had a great life. This lady was a high school principal, married, and had a set of twin girls. He felt she shouldn't have started a new family, knowing her son was out there in the world. Overall, he's an ass.

"Tessa, can I speak with you, please?" David whispered.

"If you're going to come to my house unannounced, speak up. What the hell do you want?"

"Look, you are making Jennifer's life a living hell. She didn't have anything to do with what Aubrey is claiming. She was placed on desk duty and had her gun taken away."

"Does Jennifer know you're here?"

"Tessa, I don't want you to say anything to her. I am sorry Aubrey got hurt. First, Allison didn't do anything wrong. Second,

Jennifer wasn't even around when it happened. It has been proven she was at the station. I feel like…."

"David, let me stop you before you say something you regret. You don't like me. You don't like my daughter. I don't like you, and I'm sure my daughter doesn't like you either. I don't care what Jennifer, Allison, you, or any other dirty cop is going through. Get off of my porch, now."

"Look, I'm trying to be nice, but you're not making it easy. If you don't stop, you will regret…"

"Stop before you say something you will regret. But if you choose, keep talking."

"Tessa, I'm just saying you're making a big mistake. Cops don't forget about shit like this. If Jennifer loses her job, your family will pay for it. I'm not making any threats. I'm simply letting you know how all of this works when it comes down to blue. My suggestion is you leave Jennifer out of it."

"Is that so? You know what, this conversation is over. David, get off my porch," my mother demanded as she slammed the door.

"Ma, what do you think he'll do?" I asked in a concerned voice.

"Aubrey, don't worry about him. He's a big dog with all bark and no bite. David is also a dummy. He doesn't know the doorbell camera records everything once you approach the porch. I am going to call Pamela and let her know."

Just as my mother was about to call our lawyer, her phone rang. "Girl, your ears must have been ringing. I was about to call you." My mom placed her phone on speaker so that I could hear everything.

"I have some good news for you two," Pamela spoke.

"Please give us some good news because we need it," I yelled through the phone.

"I have the tape from the store. The security company was no help, but Free called me today. She was going through some paperwork and came across an agreement she signed with the security company. Free forgot she was paying an additional $19.99 a month to have all footage stored on a different network. From the network, it's sent to the cloud. All of this time, Free had the video stored on her cloud. Of course, the security company didn't bother to remind her of this. We got them. Free emailed me the footage for that day. As we expected, there were no police or ambulance there. I wanted to tell you first, but I have a meeting with the state's attorney in an hour. No, we don't have evidence that they hit Aubrey yet, but we have them lying so far. If we can prove they lied, it will be extremely hard for anyone to believe anything they say. What do you think?"

"Girl, that is the best news we have heard all day. Now, I have something for you. Guess who visited us?" my mother added.

"Who? Did Kevin come around?"

"Kevin is not an issue. Sorry, Aubrey, I know you love your father, but he's being childish."

"Ma, please." I rolled my eyes and laid back on the couch.

"David Black stopped by my house just before you called."

"Why does that name sound familiar? Who is he?" Pamela pondered.

"His name sounds familiar because I told you about him. David Black is Captain Jennifer Black's husband. Let's just say he's not making things easy for his wife. My porch camera recorded everything. Before you ask, there is a sign on the doorbell camera that states, you are being recorded."

"What did he say?"

"He wants me to leave Jennifer out of it. David told me that I would regret it if I didn't," she explained.

"He's an idiot. Can you send me that? I am taking this to the state's attorney also. We are almost there. I will call you and let you know the results."

"Thank you," my mom and I said in unison.

Our call ended with Pamela, and I stood there speechless. I couldn't believe everything was finally coming together. My mother didn't say too much. She went into her office and shut the door. That was the last I heard from her until around 3.

"Aubrey, if you still want to look at cars, let's go."

"Say less. What dealer are we going to?"

"I was thinking Lexus. They are good starter cars, and we can find a nice used one. What do you think?" my mom answered.

"That's fine, but I thought we would go to a Honda dealer."

"Girl, bye. I cannot be driving around in a Range or Porsche, and my daughter drives a Honda. I have enough money saved to put down a nice amount to get your payments low. Plus, your father will help with the payments."

"How much do you have saved?" I inquired.

"I have almost fifteen thousand saved for your car. I have been saving since you were in middle school."

"Ma, you know you can buy a car with that amount. You don't have to worry about a car payment and insurance."

"Don't worry about it. I spoke to your dad about this a few months ago. One of us will pay the insurance and the other car payment. I will be okay if I know you're driving a safe car."

"Okay."

***

We were at the dealership for two hours. My mom said it was normal. If this is what it's like every time you buy a car, I don't want it. I walked out of the dealer with a red 2016 ES 300. Grand-Grand caught an Uber to the dealer so she could drive my car back to the house. I was hoping my mother would let me drive back. She told me I couldn't because I didn't have my license yet, and there was no other adult in the car with me.

Nevertheless, I will have a car waiting for me when I get my license. Of course, my car must be parked in the driveway because both of my mother's cars are in the garage. We went into the house to eat the crabs we picked up on the way from getting my car. To celebrate the good news Pamela gave us and me getting a car; my mom ordered three dozen crabs, a pound of steamed shrimps, corn on the cob, fried oysters, and mussels. We sat on the deck and enjoyed the sun beaming down on us. No one talked about what happened to me or any other bad thing. Music was playing, and my neighbor's dog was barking, but I felt good. Well, that is until Pamela called. Everyone froze when we saw her name pop across my mom's screen. My mother licked the old bay from her fingers, turned the music down, and slid her finger across her phone to answer it.

"Hey Pamela, do you have good news for us?" my mom asked.

"Yes, I do. There will be a news conference tomorrow morning. The state's attorney will announce the charges against Officer Brickley, Cooper, and Captain Black. Black is being charged with tampering with evidence and covering up for Cooper and Brickley. Cooper and Brickley will be charged with second-degree assault, falsifying a report, and harassment. The second-degree assault carries up to ten years and a possible fine of $25,000. Tampering with evidence is a misdemeanor. Black will probably lose her job or be given probation. I doubt if she will get jail time. The falsifying of the report and harassment charges are considered misconduct. They could lose their job, get fined, probation, stuff like that.

"The good thing about all of this is, these are good charges. We didn't want to overcharge them and end up with a mistrial. They will be required to turn themselves in within 24 hours of making the announcement. Their lawyers are being contacted now. This is good news," Pamela explained.

"What about the grand jury?" I spoke up.

"They will have to go before a grand jury. I am confident they will be indicted."

"How long will it take to get a grand jury together? How much longer will Aubrey have to deal with this? She's going back to school soon. Will they still be on duty?" Grand-Grand added.

"It could take weeks or months to put together a grand jury. I am pushing for this to move swiftly. I don't know how long Aubrey will be going through this. Even after the trial is over, she will be dealing with this. Trust me; someone out there will always remind her of what happened. And they will not be fired yet, from my understanding. I believe all three are on desk duty now. It is up to the police department whether they want to fire them. Of course, if they are charged, they will lose their job. I know this is just the beginning, but we have a lot on our side.

"Many of these cases will never have charges brought up. I am thankful for the small things. I will not be attending the press conference tomorrow. I need to spend time with my family. I don't want you guys attending either. Watch it on television. I will also be putting someone outside of your house starting tonight. I have a friend that does personal security. Believe me, when I say the media will be harassing you."

"Will he be alone?" my mom questioned.

"No, he has a team. They will rotate shifts. Wherever you go, they will go. I know it will be annoying, but I am paying him a butt load of money to make sure no one bothers your family. He'll arrive around nine tonight."

"You mean, I will be paying them a butt load of money," my mom joked.

"Well, yeah and no. I'm not charging you an additional fee for them. It's coming out of what you're currently paying me. I want to make sure you guys are safe."

"Who is he? You keep saying he, but we don't know his name," I added.

"Sorry, his name is Shawn. Shawn will bring his team by tonight and introduce you to everyone."

"Okay. Thank you for letting us know. Right now, I want to finish enjoying my evening without talking about these cops," my mom said.

For the rest of the evening, no one said anything. The music was playing, and we all tuned everything out. The three of us sat outside all evening. No breeze flowing at all. It was a hot week in August, but relaxing felt good. Finally, after all the crabs and everything else was gone, we all laid back in the reclining chairs and stared into the sky. As we enjoyed the humid air, the doorbell rang. It was exactly 9:00, and we were sure it was the security team. Grand-Grand wanted to stay out back to clean up. My mother and I went to meet them.

"Good evening, ma'am. My name is Shawn, and this is my team. May we come in?" Shawn asked.

"Sure. I'm Tessa, and this is my daughter Aubrey."

"Nice to meet you. I'm assuming you spoke with Mrs. Owens."

"Yes, we did. How does this work?" my mom questioned.

"This is Mike, Denny, Austin, Ray, and as you know, I'm Shawn. We will rotate out doing eight-hour shifts. Our job is to sit outside your house to protect your family from the media and unwanted guests. If you leave, we follow behind you. My team will not disturb you. Most of the time, you won't even know we're outside. Do you have any questions?" Shawn explained.

"Yes, I do. I mostly work in my office. What happens when I leave for work or anything else but Aubrey is home alone?"

"We will stay here with Aubrey. I believe it's better if whoever is home has someone sitting on them. Call whoever is on duty if you are at work and don't feel safe. This is a list of everyone with their number and work schedule. The shifts will not change unless an emergency comes up. I will call you and let you know if there is a change."

"How will we know you're outside? Will someone knock on the door to let us know they are leaving and someone else is on duty?" my mother continued to question.

"No. On this list is each staff car description also. There's no need to disturb you when we arrive. We will be parked in the same spot every day. We will be a few feet away from your mailbox. You need to contact me if you look outside and don't see a car."

"What about when guests arrive? Like my dad, my grandmother, or friends?" I questioned.

"That's a good question. If you know you will have guests, shoot a text to whoever is on duty and let them know who will be coming. If you can provide the car description, that would work. We don't want to harass your guest or make them uncomfortable. That's not our mission. We want to protect you, but until we get to know the normal people that will come in and out of your house, we will question them or contact you. I know this is not comfortable at all, but it's needed. Mrs. Owens told me everything that was going on. In these situations, the media will start coming around more than before. They will sit outside of your property daily. If the announcement is being made tomorrow, I'm sure someone will be at your house on Monday morning. Someone will probably be at your office also."

"That's an issue. I don't want to work from home every day."

"What about when I go back to school?"

"We will escort you to school or follow behind whoever is driving you. We don't recommend a school bus. My team will sit outside of your school until you're dismissed. If you have after-school activities, you need to let us know. If we're dropping you off, we will pick you up in a designated spot afterward. I would appreciate it if you could give us Aubrey's school schedule soon. Is that okay?"

"Yeah, that's fine. You mentioned someone being here is safer, but I don't think so. If Aubrey is left in the house alone, she's not going outside. If I leave, I don't want to walk into my office and be surrounded by media. I rather you follow me to work and any other place I go. If we both leave, whoever is on duty should leave also."

"If that is what you will like, I can make it happen," Shawn assured us.

"Thank you," my mother said as she stared Shawn down.

Since they arrived, I watched her eyes, and she hasn't taken them off, Shawn.

"Do you have any other questions?" Shawn asked.

"No. Thank you," my mother answered.

"Okay. I will be on shift tonight, and if you need anything, please call me," Shawn reminded us.

"Thank you. It was nice meeting all of you. Shawn, before you leave, can I get you some coffee or something to eat?" my mom asked in her flirtatious voice.

"No, thank you, ma'am. I have coffee, and I packed a meal."

"What about if you need to use the bathroom?" my mother probed.

"We'll be okay."

"If you ever need to use the bathroom, please don't hesitate to call and ask. We have a bathroom on the first floor, so it wouldn't be a bother."

"Thank you, ma'am. If there is nothing else, we'll allow you to enjoy the rest of your night."

Once Shawn and his team left, I turned to my mother, staring at them through the window.

"Ma, he was cute. All of them were cute," I teased.

"No, thank you. Let's go help your grandmother finish cleaning up."

When we arrived out back, Grand-Grand was lying in the hammock sleeping.

"Grand-Grand, are you staying the night?" I asked.

"I'm not asleep. I was praying. I asked God to please indict those cops and be sure they are convicted. I am about to go home and sleep in my comfortable bed. I put the trash bags in the corner. Someone needs to take them to the trash can in the garage."

"Thanks for driving Aubrey back home today."

"Don't forget I still need you to take me to the airport on Tuesday, Tessa."

"Ma, I did forget. I am glad you reminded me. What time do you need to be there?"

"I want to get there around 6:30 that morning. My flight leaves at 9:20, and you know how it is when you're flying internationally."

"Okay. Why don't you stay here Monday night so I won't have to drive to your house? You can leave your car in the driveway until you come back."

"Tessa, that's too much work. That means I have to pack all of my bags and lug them over here. When you can, swing by my house. You act like I live far," Grand-Grand protested.

"Ma, you don't make any sense at all. Either way, you will need to pack your bags and lug them somewhere."

"Tessa, you have to drive past my area to get to the airport. Arrive at my house between 5:45 and 6. That's it. Good night."

My mother wasn't happy at all. I understood what Grand-Grand was saying. But my mother didn't like it. Grand-Grand left, and I went to my room for the night. This crab smell needed to come off, and I wanted to call Bailey to let her know I finally got a car.

***

"Good morning, I know this is unusual to do a press conference on a Sunday morning, but this is an urgent matter. My office has decided to charge the following officers in the assault on teenager Aubrey Tucker. I am going to be brief. Each officer has been informed of the charges, and the next step is to gather a grand jury. I am starting with officer Lucy Cooper. Officer Cooper, who has served the department for one year, is being charged with second-degree assault, falsifying a report, and harassment. Officer Brickley, a 10-year veteran, will be charged with second-degree assault, falsifying a report, and harassment. Before I proceed with the other charges, I would like to say how disappointed I am with Officer Brickley's leadership. He was appointed as a training officer, and he should have known better. This is not how the county expects its officers to act on the job or train other officers.

"Next up is the charges for Captain Black. Even though Captain Black was not at the scene, she did play a role in how the evidence was presented. Captain Black will be charged with tampering with evidence and covering up for Cooper and Brickley. From my knowledge and evidence, Captain Black's daughter called her to inform her of what occurred in front of her door. Instead of Captain Black following protocols, she took matters into her own hands from that point. A significant amount of evidence backs up each charge. My office is confident justice will be served for Aubrey Tucker. I will not take any questions at this time due to the nature of the case. However, I would like to assure everyone that Officer Cooper,

Officer Brickley, and Captain Black have been taken off the streets, and their weapons have been turned in. Everyone is still employed as an officer of the law, but they must turn themselves in at the precinct to start the process. Each individual has been notified. Thank you for coming out, and this ends our press conference," States Attorney Laura Finway announced.

"Wow, mom, this is real. I didn't know Pamela would be there."

"Yeah, Pamela sent me a text early this morning that she would be. She also told me the States Attorney's husband is black. They have three kids, two boys and a girl. From my understanding, her oldest son, a freshman at an Ivy League school, was harassed by campus police. Pamela sent me the article this morning. I didn't hear about this in the news, but…."

"Ma, what does this have to do with my case?"

"Hold on and listen. All of this is according to the interview she did after everything happened with her son. She and her husband always gave their kids an allowance, but only if they did their chores without asking. Unlike her other kids, Jordan, the oldest, never spent his allowance money. He told his parents his first car would be a BMW from a young age. He loved BMWs, and he saved for it. Jordan saved his allowance money, birthday, Christmas, and wages from when he started working at 14. He had enough money to buy a BMW when he graduated from high school. According to her, the car was four years old but in great condition. As he drove through campus, Jordan was pulled over by campus police. They received a call that a suspicious black male was driving through the campus in a possible stolen car.

"Laura stated her husband always taught their kids what to do if the police pulled them over. He was locked up, and the car was towed. The next day Laura and her husband flew to her son, and he was released. Mysteriously when they arrived, he had a busted lip. The cops said Jordan got into a fight with a man held in the same holding cell. Jordan claimed the officer hit him when he revealed who his mother was. It was a mess. I believe this is a good thing for us. She's going to fight for justice because of what her son went through."

"I guess, but I don't want to use her trauma to help me."

"Yeah, I hear you."

"Don't forget my driver's test is scheduled for next Saturday," I reminded my mother.

"It's on my calendar. Do you want some breakfast? I was going to make some eggs and bacon."

"Sure. Oh, dad is coming to pick me up later today. They are going to the outlet, and he asked if I wanted to come."

"Who are they, Aubrey?"

"Dad, Madison, and Maddox. They are going across the bridge to the outlet. Is it okay if I go? Dad is spending money, and I am not passing up shopping."

"He's bringing that woman to my house…."

"Ma, before you continue, she's not coming in. Dad probably won't come in. Can I please go?"

"Sure. I'm going to fix breakfast. Also, check to see if the guy on duty outside would like something to eat or drink."

"No. They already said not to worry about them. Leave them alone."

"I was trying to be nice. What time is your father coming?"

"Around noon, I think. Bailey is going to come over because she's riding with us."

"Did Bailey talk to her mother about going to the outlet?"

"Of course, that's the only way dad would let her come. Before you ask, she has her own money. She's an authorized user on her mother's American Express. Can I use your credit card?"

"Girl, bye. Your father is taking you shopping, so you don't need my money."

"That is correct, but you haven't taken me shopping in a while," I stated.

"I just bought you a car. I can take it back and give you money for clothes instead."

"Say less. I'm good with the car and spending dad's money on clothes. I'm going to go upstairs and call Bailey and then get into the shower to get ready."

I was happy to spend the day with my father, even though Madison had to come. But I was going to be with Bailey, my dad, and my brother. I was looking forward to spending all of his money until I received a phone call from Allison. I wasn't sure if it was wise to answer, but I figured we both had things to say.

"You have the nerve to be calling me," I boldly said when I answered the phone.

"Aubrey, I didn't call to argue with you. I called because we need to get some things off our chest. I would love to get our friendship back to where it was. Can we talk?"

"You can talk. I don't have much to say."

"Please hear me out. I saw all of the interviews you and your mother did. I want to know, why did you lie on me? My mother could get into a lot of trouble because of your lies. I am getting harassing calls and messages on social media because everyone thinks I watched whatever happened to you. Aubrey, I didn't see anything. I was in my room putting my shoes on. By the time I got downstairs, I saw them putting you in the ambulance. I ran outside to ask the cops what happened, but they wouldn't tell me anything. That is when I called my mother."

After Allison offered her spill of lies, I didn't say anything. It seemed like the phone was silent for about five minutes. I'm sure it wasn't even a minute before she realized I wasn't going to say anything. See, I didn't trust Allison anymore. She could have been easily recording this call. No one was going to catch me slipping. My story is not going to change.

"Aubrey, can you say something? You have to believe me."

"I don't have to believe you. I know what happened to me. I don't know what you believe happened. I don't know what you want me to say. There are two things I am sure about. You stared me in the face and watched those cops harass and beat me. I also know you lied and said I never came to your house. This conversation is done."

After I said what needed to be said, I hung up on Allison. I am glad I was able to get that off my chest. Since everything happened, I always felt like something was holding me down. I was feeling lighter.

"Ma, come here, please."

"Aubrey, come down here."

"Ma, guess who just called me?"

"Who?" my mother asked in suspense.

"Allison."

Suddenly, the television was muted, and I had my mother's full attention.

"What the hell did she want? Why is she calling you? Did you answer?"

"I did answer, but I didn't say much. She tried to convince me that I was lying about saying she saw everything. The conversation didn't last more than two minutes probably. I wasn't going to say anything because I don't trust her. Do you think we should tell Pamela?"

"I am going to let her know. In the future, don't take her calls. Let her go to voicemail."

"I was about to, but I wanted to see what she had to say…."

"Hold on, that's one of the guys from outside calling me."

"They're probably calling because Bailey is here. I was supposed to be ready by now."

My mother walked to the front door and waved Bailey to the house. As our security walked her to the front door, my mom told him she was my friend.

"Ma, can you let him know dad is coming soon?"

I grabbed Bailey by the hand and pulled her up the steps. I let my mother deal with the henchmen outside.

"Girl, your house is under surveillance. Why didn't you tell me I would have to show ID to get in?" Bailey joked.

"I forgot. Our attorney thought it was wise to have someone sitting outside the house. Hoping to keep the media and anyone else away."

"That's smart. Has there been a lot of media?" Bailey questioned.

"Not really. It was before they came. Other than my neighbors being nosey, it's been quiet. What are you buying today?"

"My mother gave me the Amex card. She told me not to spend more than three thousand. You know I'm blowing Nike and Under Armour up. I need some new workout clothes. I don't know what else I want, but I know I'll spend every dime."

"I don't know how much my dad is giving me."

"When do I get to see the new car? I need more than a picture."

"It's parked in the driveway. I take my test next week."

"Oh, I did see it."

"Make yourself comfortable. I'm going to get into the shower."

***

When I finished in the shower and got dressed, my dad was parked out front. He refused to come in; honestly, their immaturity was getting on my nerves. It took us almost two hours to arrive at the outlet. We stopped twice because Maddox needed to be changed. Then we stopped again because Madison had to use the bathroom not long after we pulled out of the McDonald's parking lot. Not too long after Madison used the bathroom, we pulled over again because she had to vomit. This is when I found out she was pregnant again. Technically, my dad didn't tell me. As we were on the side of the road, ten minutes from our stop, I heard my dad tell her it was almost over. The first trimester is always hard. I know I'm going to love the next one just as much as I love Maddox, but another baby was too much. My father is getting old.

Once we arrived at the mall, my dad handed me a $100.00 Visa gift card that my uncle Craig left for me before returning home. Along with the gift card, he gave me $2,000.00 in cash. Bailey and I left the adults and tore the outlet up. Even though we wore uniforms to school, I needed clothes for the weekend, shoes, purses, and tennis shoes. With the stuff from the outlet and my mother, I'll be set until Christmas. We went to the Adidas store and got matching jackets, and I bought a few sports bras. I'm not a big fan of Coach, but Bailey wanted a new waist bag. We both wanted some perfume from Michael Kors. I went in there for perfume but ended up buying a watch also. We stopped in Nike, Polo, and Under Armour. They didn't have as many stores as I thought. We usually go to Clarksburg or Tanger. I know I'll never come back here. I tried to spend all of my money but I couldn't. It wasn't much to buy.

I don't think we were there for more than two hours, but I enjoyed being with Bailey. However, I still wonder why I never chose her as my best friend. What was it about Allison? Why did I choose her as a best friend over Bailey? If I had never befriended Allison, none of this would have happened.

"Aubrey, did you hear me?" my dad asked.

"Huh! What happened?"

"Aubrey, are you okay? I asked you twice if you were okay with eating at Red Robin."

"Oh, sorry. I was daydreaming. Yes, Red Robin is cool. Can we stop at the one in Columbia? I still have some money left. I want to get some stuff from Hollister and Hot Topic."

"Yeah, that's fine. Madison, do you mind stopping at the mall?"

"Babe, I really would like to go home. I don't even want to eat," Madison whined.

She thought I didn't hear her. The whispering didn't work. I saw my dad look in the mirror at me. I made sure my face was screwed up.

"Madison, I can drop the girls off at the mall. Once I drop them off, I'll have enough time to order the food to go and pick them up. We'll be home in no time."

"Madison, I will make sure I am in and out. I know what you may be going through with the pregnancy and all," I sarcastically added.

"Brey…"

"Madison, my name is not Brey. My parents named me Aubrey."

"I'm sorry, I just like that as a nickname. Anyway, I'm not pregnant. Where would you get that idea?"

By now, Bailey is giving me the side-eye. My dad is giving Madison the side-eye, and I am about to catch her in a lie.

"Madison, you are pregnant. I heard my dad saying something about the first trimester. I am almost an adult; you don't have to lie to me. You two having another baby has nothing to do with me. Dad, can you drop us off at the mall? If it's too much trouble with picking us up, I'll call mom."

At that moment, the car was silent. No one said anything. Madison had an attitude because I got my way. My dad placed the mall address in his GPS, and Madison wasn't happy. In almost an hour, my dad dropped us off at the mall and made his way to pick up the food.

"Girl, you are a spoiled brat," Bailey joked.

"I am, but my father can't have my mother mad at him and me. He knows I'll go home and tell my mother. He also knows she would cuss him out. Madison will only whine, and then he'll buy her something. Plus, she lied about being pregnant. My dad may not tell me something right away, but he doesn't lie to me. She'll be fine."

"You're not afraid that when the new baby comes, your dad won't give in as much?"

"No. Look, my dad knows how much the divorce hurt me. He also knows I don't like Madison and never will. I tolerate her for his sake and Maddox."

"I didn't tell you that I saw my dad," Bailey revealed.

"What! I never heard you talk about him."

"Outside of my family, no one knows about my dad. My dad was in prison for aggravated assault and property damage. He got out last month. He was sentenced to 10 years but only did eight because of good behavior. A couple of months before we moved, my dad beat a man with a bat along with, busting his car windows out. My dad has a twin, my Aunt Kelly. My aunt was always saving herself for marriage. She met this man at church who said he was okay with it. It turned out he wasn't. They had been dating for about a month when she invited him over for dinner. We had met him and everything. Everyone thought they were a good match. That night after dinner, he raped her. After the rape, he left as if nothing had happened. I was young, but I still knew everything that was going on. Adults always talked around me.

"My aunt called my dad from the hospital. He went to the man's house, but the guy wouldn't come out. My dad started busting his car windows. The guy came out immediately. That's when my dad beat him. He broke his arm and leg with the bat. Then he busted his lip along with, giving him a black eye with his fist. Afterward, my dad called the police and turned himself in. My parents weren't married, but they were engaged. My dad lost everything. He was a plumber and had plans to start his business.

"When he was sentenced, he and my mom agreed I wouldn't see him in prison. I always talked to him, and he sent me letters and pictures. My dad going to prison is the biggest reason we moved to Texas. My mother didn't want to stay here because of the rumors. I'm sure if you ask your mother about it, she'll tell you the story. According to my mother, everyone in the county knew about it. It's funny how rumors travel. The incident happened in another county. My mother sought out a new job in Texas.

"My dad is out of prison and staying with my aunt and her family. I want my parents to get back together, but I know it's not going to happen. Even though my mother never married and barely dated, they are awkward around each other. Aubrey, I haven't seen or touched my father in eight years. He looks the same, except for the grey hair, but I don't know him. I have talked to my father a couple of times a week since he left. But seeing him is different. I don't know how to act around him. I missed him, but how do I build that relationship with him? I asked my mother if he could stay with us, and she said it wasn't up to her. My dad's pride is getting in the way. He doesn't have a job and refuses to be a burden. My aunt feels like it was all her fault, so she's not letting him leave," Bailey confessed.

"Wow, I can't imagine what you're going through. The only thing I can say is to try and build something with him slowly. If you want to, talk to my mom. Her father, my grandfather, was in prison. That's why my grandmother divorced him. He went to prison for selling drugs. He was sentenced to 10 years when my mother was 7. My mother told me he came home just in time for her high school graduation. She tried to build a relationship with him, but it was hard.

"My mom said things started coming together when she went off to college. He would come down to the school and visit her. When she came home, they spent time together and everything. She said there was always a question about where he was getting so much money because he didn't work. How could he travel, help pay for tuition, and buy her things? Towards the end of her freshman year, he was locked up again for check and credit card fraud. My grandfather was sentenced to 35 years in prison. He died from a heart attack after being there for three years.

"My mother said when he was in prison the first time; my grandmother never let her go see him. He could only write letters because my grandmother wouldn't accept his collect calls. I said all that to say, my mother knows what you're going through. Call my mother if you ever want to speak with someone who went through it."

"Thanks. I'll think about it."

Chapter 7: "Senior Year"

Summer break is over and today is the first day of my senior year. I got my license which means I can drive myself to school. The only part that sucked was having a detail behind me, but I will say, Mr. Denny stayed behind so he wouldn't be obvious. He reminds me of my dad. Mr. Denny is laid back and down to Earth. I asked him if I could stop at Chick Fil A, and he agreed, even though we aren't supposed to make any stops that weren't previously on the schedule.

When my mom received my schedule in the mail, she called my school to verify if I would have any classes with Allison. She told them it wouldn't be a good idea with everything going on. I told my mother I would be okay. She is on the on the cross-country team with me. We were bound to cross paths anyway. The administration told her they couldn't reveal Allison's schedule, but everyone would keep an eye on us if we were in the same class.

Bailey and Zyair agreed to meet me at the bottom of the steps this morning. Zyair had a crush on Bailey, and even though he's younger than us, I think she likes him too.

"Hey, sis, how did it feel driving to school in your new car?" Zyair asked as he hugged me.

"It felt good. Are ya'll ready for a new school year?" I responded.

"Hell yeah. Look, Aubrey, we only have two classes together, but text me if anyone bothers you," Bailey said.

"I'll be good. If there are any issues, I only have to text my security detail, and his big ass will be in here expeditiously, as my boy T.I. would say."

"Yo, you have a security detail. Okay, big time," Zyair joked.

"Nah, because of all of the attention my family has been getting, we needed it. They just want to make sure I'm safe."

My friends and I walked up the stairs to enter the building. It was senior year, and this was going to be epic. When I walked into the building, the first person I saw was Officer Sheppard. I stopped in my tracks and felt like my chicken biscuit was about to come up. Even though we attend a private school, we do have security. They placed her here five years ago because of all the mass shootings in schools. She's cool, but I no longer trust her. I stood there as Bailey and Zyair walked ahead of me. I don't even think they realized I was no longer walking.

"Aubrey, are you coming?" Bailey stated as she turned around.

Tears started rolling down my cheeks, and I turned around to go back outside. Mr. Denny must have seen me walking back down the steps. He was parked across the street from the entrance. I saw him get out of the car and start running towards me. I ran down the steps and heard Bailey and Zyair calling my name. I wanted to turn around, but I couldn't. Mr. Denny met me in the middle of the steps.

"Aubrey, are you okay? What happened?"

"I can't go in there," I cried.

"Yo, Aubrey, what's going on? Are you okay?" Bailey questioned.

"You two go ahead to class. She'll be okay. I'll handle it," Mr. Denny demanded.

Zyair and Bailey walked back into the school, and Mr. Denny walked me to the bottom of the stairs.

"Do you need me to call your mother?"

"No. She'll come up here and start acting all motherly and crazy."

"That sounds like your mother," Mr. Denny laughed. The crew has gotten to know my family pretty well. Even though Mr. Shawn insisted they didn't need food or use the bathroom, we bent those rules several times, especially when Mr. Shawn was the first to ask to use the bathroom.

'What happened?"

"We have a cop in our school. Officer Sheppard, she's cool. She's a very nice black lady, but seeing her in the uniform made me have flashbacks. Every time I see a cop, I start to panic."

"That's normal. Have you gone back to therapy? I remember your mom saying you didn't want to go."

"I went last week because she made me, but it doesn't help."

"Will it help if I walked you in the building every day?"

"No, because all attention will be on me."

"How about I walk you in today? I'll have a small chat with the officer while you head to class."

"Okay."

Mr. Denny walked me to the front door, and all eyes were on me. There were still students coming in and some standing in the hallway. The bell hadn't rung yet. I saw Bailey and Zyair standing near the elevators. I'm glad they waited for me. I left Mr. Denny standing there talking to Officer Sheppard. I don't know what he was saying to her, but she was blushing.

"Hey girl, are you okay?" Bailey asked as she hugged me.

"Yeah. I get nervous when I see cops," I explained.

"You know Sheppard is cool. She wears the badge, but she's not like them," Bailey assured me.

"I know. Come on, let's go to homeroom," I suggested.

All three of us got on the elevator to go upstairs. We were all in different homerooms, but they were all on the second floor. My coach would kill me if she found out I used the elevator instead of the stairs. Bailey and I homeroom were next door to each other. Zyair's were around the corner in the east wing with the other eleventh graders. As soon as I walked into my homeroom, the two people I didn't want to see were already in their seats. Jason and Allison. One of my favorite English teachers, Mrs. Sanders, was my homeroom teacher. She was one of the few black teachers in the school. I was in her AP English class during my junior year. Lucky for me, she didn't do assigned seats. I found a seat far away from those two.

Our classes were always small, with no more than 16 students. And 16 was a lot. Jason was sitting towards the back of the class, and Allison was sitting two seats in front of him. I chose to sit near the window. I took my phone out to text Bailey as I waited for the bell to ring.

"Girl, you wouldn't believe who's in my homeroom…."

"I already know. That bitch A."

"Yup, and Jason."

"Stop it."

"I'm going to act like they don't even exist. Especially his punk ass."

"Already. He's dead to Zy and me."

Before I could respond to Bailey, the bell rang. I remember last year when the bell rang, Mrs. Sanders didn't play about being on the phone. She was cool but also strict. I knew I would see Bailey during lunch. After lunch, we have Trigonometry and AP World History together.

Mrs. Sanders did her normal routine of introducing herself and explaining her class expectations. We were 15 minutes into the class, and Officer Sheppard interrupted our class time.

"Excuse me, but can I see Aubrey Tucker in the hall? I'll be quick."

"Sure, Officer Sheppard," Mrs. Sanders responded.

I had no idea what this lady wanted. I went into the hall, and she closed the door behind me. I always thought she was cool until this moment.

"Hey Aubrey, how was your summer?"

"Good."

"I am glad school is open because, during the summer, I have to do patrol work."

"No disrespect, but I know you didn't pull me out of class to talk about summer break."

"You're right. I wanted to talk to you about this morning. Denny told me about you being nervous because I'm a cop. I wanted to let you know there is nothing to worry about. I got your back, Sis."

"Okay," I stated in a confused but annoyed tone. "Is that all?"

"Yes, but if you ever need anything, let me know. I don't know Denny personally, but I found out he knows my brother. They went to high school together."

"Why are you telling me this?"

"My bad. I just wanted to let you know that you don't have to be afraid of me. I'm not like the rest of them. I believe you when you say they beat you. Between you and me, it happens all the time. I hope they don't get away with it."

"Okay, thank you. Anything else?"

"No. I just wanted to let you know; that you're safe here. If anyone gives you any trouble, come talk to me."

"Okay," I stated and walked back into class.

When I arrived back in class, Mrs. Sanders was still explaining her rules and expectations. We only stayed in homeroom for 30 minutes, and I was happy when the bell rang. My first period was Chemistry, and as I walked down the hall, it felt like everyone was staring at me. At first, I thought I was being dramatic like they do in the movies. They're slowly walking down the hall, and everything is in slow motion. All the kids are standing up against the lockers, whispering as if the back of my uniform skirt was filled with shit. The only thing is, I wasn't imagining things. Not everyone but a few students were standing around whispering about me and not making it discreet. I ignored them and kept going. When I arrived in Chemistry, Jason came in behind me. Just my luck, my teacher Mr. Levi gave us assigned seats. Jason and I are sitting next to each other.

"Hey Aubrey, how are things going?" Jason asked.

"Good." I figured he would leave me alone if I gave him a one-word answer. I was wrong.

"Look, I know I messed up over the summer. Can we please talk? I miss you, and if you would give me a chance, I will show you I'm sorry."

"I'm good."

"Stop acting like you don't miss me."

Deep down, I was missing him. I was trying hard not to show it, but he was sitting next to me with the biggest smile on his face showing off his white teeth. I took one look at the waves in his hair, and I gave him.

"Look, we can talk, but I'm not making any promises. Today is my first day back at practice. We can either talk after practice, or you can call me tonight."

"Say less."

I missed the first two weeks of cross-country practice because my mom convinced Dr. Chambers, I needed more time to heal. We always start practice at least two weeks before school starts. He told her I was okay with running, but she said no. His note back to school said I could resume all physical activity today. I had a lot of catching up to do, but at least I'm still captain. I wasn't looking forward to having Allison on my team. Unfortunately, it wasn't my choice.

I wished my school did half days for seniors like public schools did. After Chemistry, I was drained. Mr. Levi had us do work on the first day and gave us homework. After Chemistry, there was my foreign language class and a mini college prep class that was pointless to me. According, to our class counselor, they added this class for the first semester and then again in the third semester to make sure all seniors were ready for college. After that class was lunch, Trigonometry, and my last class was AP World History.

"Girl, I'm so glad your mother let you practice," Bailey stated as we walked to the locker room.

"Me too. How has practice been?"

"You know, Coach. She had us running hills during the first week. I know she's tough, but I didn't expect it to be that so soon."

"Did anyone ask about me?" I questioned.

"No, but I did overhear some whispers between Allison and Emma. Emma told Allison she should ask Coach if she could be captain since you weren't able to return. When they saw me, both of them shut up."

"Typical, but Coach told my mother I was still captain. Allison wish could be me. She doesn't stand a chance in beating me out as team captain. She can chill."

"No one is worried about them. You're good, and neither of them will step to you. Come on, so we can change."

***

Our practice was almost two hours, and the sun didn't help. After I slipped on my sweatpants, Bailey and I walked toward our car. Like I figured, Mr. Denny was standing in front of his car waiting for me.

"Aubrey, wait up," Jason yelled from the school steps.

"Do you want me to wait with you?" Bailey asked.

"No, go ahead home. He just wants to talk. I'll call you later."

I stopped to talk to Jason, and just before he reached me, my phone rang. It was Mr. Denny.

"Hello," I answered.

"Are you okay, Aubrey?"

"Yes. My friend wanted to talk to me after practice," I responded.

"You'll have to tell your friend you two will talk later. My shift ends in 30 minutes, which means I need to get you home to fill in Austin."

"Okay," I stated as I ended the call.

"Hey Jason, can I call you when I get home? I have to leave."

"Is everything okay? I thought you said we could talk after practice. I waited around for you."

"My security told me I can't stay behind," I confessed as I nodded toward Mr. Denny.

"Security?"

"Yeah, with everything going on, my attorney hired security to keep me safe."

"Homeboy been out here all day?" Jason laughed.

"Yeah, that's what he gets paid for."

"Ard! I'll call you later. Can I walk you to your car?"

"Where's your car?" I asked.

"I parked in the back of the parking lot. I got here late, and all of the spaces up front were gone."

"You can walk me."

"I see you drove to school in style with your security. That Yukon is nice."

"Yeah, his truck is nice, but I drove my car. I have a Lexus."

"Damn shorty. I need to see this ride."

"I can show you, but we can't talk long. I need to leave."

"No problem."

Jason walked me to my car. Our short distance was fun. I missed his jokes and silly spirit. I showed him my car, he hugged me and went to his Camaro. His parents bought him a brand-new Camaro right before our junior prom. He loves that car.

As I pulled into the driveway, my mother was standing outside talking to Mr. Austin. When Mr. Denny parked, my mother made her way to the front door. My two bodyguards chatted, and then Mr. Denny drove off.

"Hey baby, how was school?"

"It was cool. Before you ask, nothing happened. Everything was okay."

"With the exception of you crying when you saw Officer Sheppard."

"So, Mr. Denny told you."

"Yes, that's his job. Are you okay?"

"Yes! I was just shook. Trust me, I am good. How was your work day?"

"It was pretty calm. Not too busy. I have some good news for you."

"What is it?"

"I spoke with Pamela today. First, a restraining order was put into place against David. He's also suspended with no pay while they investigate the video of him 'encouraging' me to leave Jennifer out of it."

"That is some good news. Maybe that's why Allison was giving me the side-eye all day."

"Probably not. I found that out about an hour ago. Enough about him; we have a new witness that saw everything."

"Who? On top of the tape from the boutique?"

"You now Mrs. Wolfe that lives across the street from Allison?"

"Yes, the older white lady. She was outside, or was it caught on tape? I didn't see anyone."

"From what she told Pamela, Mrs. Wolfe was standing in her doorway when she saw you walking towards Allison's house. Mrs. Wolfe said she shut her door and went to walk towards her kitchen until she heard sirens. She walked back towards the front door. Mrs. Wolfe stood in the doorway for a couple of minutes until she saw Cooper hit you. Once she saw you fall to the ground, Mrs. Wolfe stepped onto her porch. She told Pamela everything just like you said. Mrs. Wolfe even said Brickley turned around and looked her right in the face."

"Oh my gosh. I wonder why she came forth."

I was elated because this is what I needed for all of this to be over.

"Mrs. Wolfe said she was afraid to say anything because she lived alone. She didn't want any trouble. Since her husband died last year, only her daughter and grandchildren come over. She kept what she saw to herself until the news conference aired. Mrs. Wolfe immediately called her daughter. She had been having bad dreams about what she saw. Her daughter convinced her to say something. Mrs. Wolfe said she hesitated because Jennifer lived across the street. And today, she finally had the courage to contact Pamela. Her daughter found Pamela's office information. The best thing is the doorbell camera recorded everything. She didn't even think about that.

Her daughter reminded her that her doorbell was a camera. This is almost over."

"I hope so," I whispered.

"What's wrong?"

"I just feel like even with all of this evidence, they are still cops. They might not be indicted."

"I know. That's the type of world we live in. How about I cook dinner and you call your father with the news? I know he would love to hear about it."

"Oh, by the way, I'm staying with daddy this weekend," I revealed.

"Is that right?"

"Madison will be out of town for a relative's funeral. Daddy asked if I wanted to stay with him."

"So, the only reason you're staying is because Madison will not be there?"

"Ma, no! You know I can stay there anytime; I choose not to. Madison didn't want to take Maddox, so he's staying home with dad. He knows I don't like staying there with her. When I talked to him last night, he told me about her going out of town and asked if I wanted to come over. He's going to meet me here when I get out of school Friday."

"That's fine with me."

I left my mother standing in the dining room. I could tell she was bothered by me staying with my father. I wasn't going to let her anger at him keep me from having fun. I went to my room, took off my clothes, and took a shower. After my shower, I called Jason instead of doing my chemistry homework. I facetimed Jason twice, and there was no answer. After he didn't answer, I sent Jason a text message.

"WYD!!!!!"

"Aubrey, I can't talk to you. I'll tell you tomorrow."

His text response was weird, but whatever was going on with him wasn't going to keep me awake all night.

***

Weeks had passed since school started, and today the grand jury will choose if those dirty cops will be indicted. My mom asked me if I wanted to stay home from school. I told her no. I knew there would be unwanted attention, but I'm tough. If I could survive a beat down, I can continue to survive the dirty looks and words from these stuck-up ass prep kids. I was sitting in Trigonometry when my mom sent me the text message.

"We got them."

"Did they get indicted?"

"All three. We're going to celebrate tonight. Your dad was here."

"YESSSSSS! Will you be home when I get out of school?"

"Yeah. I took the day off."

After my mom sent me a text, my dad sent a GIF of Beyonce dancing. I instantly knew what it meant. He told me he'd see me later. I then sent Bailey a text letting her know. I wish I could have told Jason. The last time we talked, he told me his parents forbid him to see me. I fought to get my parents to give him a chance. But his parents think I'll do nothing but bring the weed smoker trouble. They threatened to take his car from him. Jason loves that car, but I guess he wouldn't fight for me as I did for him.

After Trigonometry, Allison must have heard the news because she was seen crying with one of her friends in the corner. Am I supposed to feel sorry for her? I think not. Fuck her! I googled the indictment, and every charge the state's attorney was going after, she got. When the state's attorney filed the charges, Mrs. Jennifer was only placed on desk duty at the time. Brickley and Cooper were arrested but made bail the same day. According to the news article from today, both of them were taken into custody after the indictment. I didn't read if Allison's mom was fired or what would happen to her. Now I hope it doesn't take forever for them to go to trial.

The end of the day finally came. Bailey and I were walking to the locker room to get ready for practice, and that's when it started. As we got closer to the locker room, this girl named Cailey put her middle finger up at me. Since everything happened, she and Allison became close. At one point, Allison didn't like her. Now they're best friends. I laughed at her, and Bailey gave her two middle fingers.

When I got to my locker to change, "NIGGA BITCH" was written there. I stood there and started crying. Bailey grabbed her towel from her locker to wipe it off, but I stopped her.

"Don't wipe it off. I'm taking a picture to send to my parents and lawyer. Go get Coach for me."

Allison, Bridgett, and Amelia were already there when we walked into the locker room. We knew one of them did it, but there was no proof.

"Aubrey, do not touch your locker. I will call the administration and security down," Coach instructed.

Coach then told everyone to meet her on the field and not get changed. All of the school authorities came down, writing stuff in their tablets and whispering to each other. Our headmistress told Coach she would talk to everyone that entered the locker room before me. There are no cameras in the locker room, but there's one at the gym entrance. It points to the locker room door and the gym overall.

The message wasn't there yesterday, so it had to happen sometime today. Head Mistress Miller let me know she would also call my parents. She didn't know I had already told them. My mom and dad were blowing up my phone. I sent them a text letting them know I was okay and would call them after practice. Mr. Shawn came to school with me today. When I got to the field to see what Coach had planned, Mr. Shawn was standing there waiting for me.

"Aubrey, are you okay? Your mom sent me a text," Shawn asked.

"Yeah. My coach wants to see us. You can stay here just in case, but I'm good for now."

"All right, I'm going to keep this simple. I don't know who thought it was okay to write 'nigga bitch' on Aubrey's locker. The one thing I don't tolerate on this team is racism. I have been a coach for over 15 years and have never experienced anything like this. I know for a fact someone from this team did it. When I came in this afternoon, the locker room was locked. This is only for athletes, and I unlocked the door when I came in. I don't know who it was, but I heard some of you girls coming into the locker room. I didn't think anything of it because it's the normal process. Either someone will confess, or we will see who came in before Aubrey. Whoever it was that came in before her will be heavily investigated. You can be down for your teammates, or someone can confess. This is not the time to unify and not speak up. I'll wait."

Coach Mona was a black woman who graduated from Liberty Prep long ago. She also made it to the Olympics and brought home the silver in the 10,000 meters. She's been coaching for a while but has been at Liberty Prep for eight years. Prior she was coaching at a city school. I like Coach Mona, but she wasn't my homegirl. None of the black girls on the team received extra attention because we were the same color. She did her job training us, kept us in line, and went home.

"Coach, how do we know Aubrey didn't do it herself?" Emma asked.

"Why would she?" Coach Mona responded.

"I mean, she is the center of attention right now. Everyone knows what happened today. She has been lying for months about everything. What makes you think she's not lying now."

"Emma, I don't have a reason to lie. I'm sure you were the one who did it since you and your homegirl were trying to take my spot as captain," I retorted.

"Sister girl…"

"Bitch don't call me sister girl because I will…."

"Girls, stop it! Emma, don't start with throwing the accusations. If you didn't do it, keep your mouth shut," Coach interrupted.

"You cannot talk to me like that. I will call my mom," Emma whined.

"Call her. While you're at it, let your mom know that I kicked you off the team. Get off my field and have a nice evening. Does anyone else want to try me?"

Emma didn't even say anything. Instead, she just walked off the field and headed to the locker room.

"Now, I want each of you to sit on the bench. I will speak with you one on one. If no one tells me, I will suspend the team's season until we find out. First up is Lana."

Lana was a ninth-grader. This was her first year at Liberty Prep. She came from a public school but received a scholarship for running. I didn't know anything about her, so I doubted if it was her. I wish I could have heard their conversation, but Coach kept everything on the hush. I only saw her writing stuff down.

"Bailey, it's your turn," Coach yelled.

I knew it wasn't Bailey because we were together. I felt like Coach was wasting her time by asking her. But I knew she had to be fair. They were talking longer than she spoke to Lana.

"Elizabeth, you're next."

Elizabeth was a junior, and she never cared for me. I don't know what I did to her, but she always carried an attitude when I told her to do something for the team's sake. Normally, I would blame her because of how she felt about me—this time, I couldn't. Elizabeth was walking behind us as we came into the gym.

"Marie-Sky, it's your turn."

Marie-Sky was another white girl I was cool with. I knew she didn't like Allison. Allison tried to talk to her boyfriend at the start of our junior year. Even though they had their issues, I didn't have a problem with Marie-Sky. I don't see her doing it, but white people tend to stick together.

"Hailey, come see me."

Hailey is a senior also. She lives two doors down from me. Hailey's dad is black, and her mom is Latino. Like Blacks, there aren't many Latinos that go to our school. Even though we lived on the same street, we were cordial. Hailey is quiet and doesn't say much to anyone outside her boyfriend, Javier. Her parents did come down to check on me when everything came out. Our moms are cool with each other. Our dads used to play basketball together in their backyard before the divorce happened. I don't think she did it, but I don't trust anyone that came into the locker room before me.

"Allison, you're up next."

Of course, I suspected Allison. She was definitely in the locker room before me with Emma. Unfortunately, their conversation didn't last more than two minutes.

"Hanna, come see me."

Hanna is also a white girl, but she's a sophomore. I don't know too much about her. Outside of running, we don't say anything to each other. What I know about Hanna is that her dad is a cop working under Mrs. Jennifer. I found that out through Allison last school year. One day I asked Allison if she wanted to come over to study for our test. Allison told me she couldn't because they were having dinner guests. The next morning, Allison told me Hanna showed up at her house with her parents. That's when she found out her dad was a cop. I'm pretty sure she hates my guts. She's suspect!

"Mae, please come here."

Mae was a junior who joined the team this year. I know her because we play softball together. I thought we were cool, but sometimes you can't tell with these white people. I wouldn't put it past her, though.

"Jae-Marie, you're the last person. Come here."

Jae-Marie was also a junior. We have known each other since third grade. Her parents are my mom's clients. Her mother is a professor, and her dad works in cyber security for the Government. They live in our development also. Jae-Marie lives in between my house and Allison's. Our moms have hung out together, so I don't know why Jae-Marie would do it, but she's white.

"Sorry, Aubrey, I need to speak with you also."

I didn't understand why she had to speak to me. I am the one that reported the crime.

"Aubrey, I'm going to speak with you like everyone else. Who did you walk into the gym with?"

"Bailey."

"When did you notice the writing on your locker?"

"As soon as I reached my locker."

"Have you had any issues with anyone?"

"With everything going on, Allison and I are no longer friends. Emma never said anything directly to me, but I heard she was trying to become captain. She has been giving me dirty looks since school started. Elizabeth never liked me, but we never had a falling out. I don't have an issue with anyone else on the team. Outside of the team, I have been getting dirty looks from a lot of girls in the school."

"Okay, thank you."

Coach and I walked back to the track where the rest of the team was standing. By now, we had been out there for almost an hour.

"Practice is suspended for today. Tomorrow, you will meet me on the track at our normal time. Come prepared to practice, but I can't guarantee we will. I will leave it at that. Go home."

I told Mr. Shawn I would meet him out front after I got my stuff from the locker room. No one said anything as we headed back into the building. When I reached my locker, it was already cleaned off. Bailey and I walked out together, and Mr. Shawn was waiting at my car. Now I had to go home and be questioned by my parents.

* * *

"Ma, I'm home," I yelled from the garage door entrance.

"Hey, are you good?" my father asked as he walked from the kitchen.

"What are you doing here?"

"I told your mom when we were at the courthouse I would go to dinner with you two. Well, she invited me."

"She invited you?" I questioned.

"Yeah! We're good. We had a conversation, and I'll leave it at that. What happened today?"

"Where's mommy? I rather not tell you and have to say it all over again."

"No need to repeat yourself. I'm right here," my mom stated as she walked up behind me.

"I don't know who did it. When I walked into the locker room with Bailey, I saw what I sent you on my locker. Security and Head Mistress came down to investigate. Coach took everyone on the field and interviewed each of us individually. Then she told us she'll see us tomorrow."

157

"Do you know who may have done it?" my dad questioned.

"Allison, Emma, or Elizabeth. None of them like me. Hopefully, they will find out soon."

"Well, I told your Head Mistress that if they don't do something, I will file my investigation and bring in the media."

"Ma, no more media. I have to go to school there. Can you let the school handle it?"

"No, because they are not going to do anything. They will say they couldn't find out who did it, but it'll be an ongoing investigation. I am not letting whoever did this get away with it."

"For once, I have to agree with your mother, Aubrey. Nothing will ever get resolved if we stand by and let them try to sweep it under the rug. Outside of this issue, how is school?"

"School is fine."

"Are you sure?" Dad continued to press the issue.

"Yes. Outside of the dirty looks, some kids give me, I'm fine."

"If you weren't, would you tell me?"

"Yes, dad. Where are we going to eat?"

"Wherever you want to go," my mom added.

"Can we go to Sully's Steakhouse?"

"Oh, you're trying to hurt my pockets," my dad joked.

"I haven't had any steak in a while. Plus, I love their bread."

"That settles it. Are we ready to go?" my mom asked.

"I need to freshen up from school. Give me about 45 minutes."

"Why do you need that long?"

"Ma, I am not wearing this uniform to dinner. It's only after 6. They don't close until 10. We have time."

I went upstairs to my room to shower and change my clothes. After I got out of the shower, I saw that Bailey had called me. I didn't know if it was important or not. I didn't want to talk to her while in the car with my parents. Knowing I couldn't talk long, there was no need to call now.

"Hey, OMW to dinner with the old people. What's up?"

"I was wondering if you heard anything about the incident today."

"Nah. My mom said if they don't do anything, she will file an investigation."

"Oh, shit. For real. Well, I hope they find out. Call me later."

***

Dinner was surprisingly great. My parents didn't argue. They talked to each other more than me. On the way home, my mom received a call from our lawyer. Allison's mom was suspended without pay pending a further investigation through the police department.

"Why are they still investigating her? They clearly know she lied and covered up the evidence. I don't get this. It's straight bull," my mom yelled through the car speaker.

"I know, Tessa, but that's how the system works. I talked to an insider I have with the police department, and they are saying most likely she will be fired. But the thing is, she can be fired and hired somewhere else as an officer."

"If your insider is saying she'll be fired, what are they waiting for?"

"Tessa, this is how it works. Let them go through the process of dealing with her. Honestly, I don't care what they do to her. I am more worried about the other two. That's what we need to focus on. I will burn their assess so much their great-great-great-grandchildren will know not to mess with another black child."

"I guess you're right. What about the civil suit?"

"We're still going for that. Trust me. I got this. I only wanted to let you know she was suspended. They didn't let me know that until about an hour ago. I'll talk to you tomorrow."

"Okay."

"Oh, by the way. I'm putting my own pressure on the school to find out who did that to Aubrey's locker today. I have a meeting with the headmistress tomorrow," Pamela revealed.

"Thanks."

We got home close to midnight, and Madison was blowing my dad's phone up. She was whining as usual about why he was out so late with my mother. She always forgets that I'm there also. When we arrived at the house, Mr. Ray was pulling up for his night shift. Before we left home, my mom told Mr. Shawn he could leave. She wanted us to go to dinner without anyone following us.

Mr. Ray didn't say too much. He wasn't like Mr. Shawn or Mr. Denny. They talked to us and acted like they enjoyed their job. Mr. Ray was an older man who stuck to the rules. He wouldn't come in to use the bathroom and barely spoke. I guess that's why he was only on the night shift. I think I only had one encounter with him, and that was one night when we came in late. He was angry with my mom for speeding back home. He told her that he had lost her a couple of times and she needed to slow down. He also works only two nights a week. My mom thinks he's retired military or law enforcement. We never asked if that was true. Mr. Mike only came twice. His wife had a baby the first week they all started. Mr. Shawn said he'll be back next week.

My dad left, and we went into the house. We both were so tired that we didn't even realize the noose hanging in the tree in our front yard until Mr. Ray knocked on the door. We were on our way up the steps when the knocking started. My mom was shocked because she knew it wasn't my dad. It had to be Mr. Ray because he wouldn't allow anyone onto our property.

"Hi, Mr. Ray. Is everything okay? Do you need to go to the bathroom?" my mom questioned.

"No, ma'am. Did you notice the tree in your front yard? Was that there when you left home this evening?"

We both looked at the tree, and that's when we saw it. The only thing I saw was tears coming from my mother's eyes. Then, she walked outside to remove it.

"No, please don't touch it. I have already called the police to make a report. I know they aren't going to do anything, but we want it in writing that it was reported. I sent a picture and message to Shawn and Mrs. Owens. Once the police come, they will remove it and use it for whatever evidence they need. Well, at least that's what they are supposed to do. I want you, young lady, to go to sleep because you have school in the morning. Your mother and I will deal with this."

"He's right, Aubrey. There's no point in you staying awake."

"Do you want me to call dad?"

"No. Madison is already acting like the brat she is. If I call him, he'll turn around. I don't want any trouble for him tonight. I'll tell him in the morning and explain why I didn't call."

***

I don't know what time my mom went to sleep last night. I took a shower and closed my eyes as soon as my head hit the pillow. When my alarm went off this morning, I heard voices coming from downstairs. I thought I was still sleeping because one of those voices was my dad.

"Good morning," I said.

"Hey, sweetheart," my mom responded.

"Dad, why are you here so early? What's going on?"

"Your mom told me what happened. I stopped by to see what was going on before going to work. Are you okay?"

"Yeah. Do we know who did it?"

"Yes and no. I guess they didn't know about the camera above your window."

"Who was it?" I questioned. Why was she leaving me in suspense?

"I think it was David, but the person had a ski mask covering their face. The man was the same height and body frame. I don't know if he was watching us when we left. But it shows that he did it 10 minutes after we pulled off. I sent a copy of the video to Pamela. It's early, so we're still waiting to hear back from her. So go ahead and get ready for school."

"Maybe we should have let Mr. Shawn stay at the house," I said.

"Maybe."

"Wow! They are acting like this."

"Look, let me know if you need to stay home."

"Nah, I'm good. Dad, what time are you leaving?"

"Probably within the next 30 minutes. I have to be at work by 8:00."

"Do you think you could fix me a breakfast bagel before you leave? Please!" I asked before going back upstairs.

"Sure."

"I think she should stay home from school today. With everything going on, Kevin, it's a lot. She's trying to be brave, but this is a lot. It's a lot for me, and I'm grown," my mom whispered.

"I agree, but we can't force her. Maybe school is a distraction for her. Trust me; if Aubrey wants to skip school, she'll let you know. I'm going to fix her breakfast."

"I wish she would stick with therapy. She'll go and then stop. Aubrey is not mentally prepared to fight this alone."

"Tessa, she's not alone. Aubrey has a whole army of supporters, including us. I know therapy is important, but it's not for everyone. It may not be her thing. Or at least not right now."

"I know, but I'm so worried about her."

My mom was partially right. This was a lot for me to handle, but I'm Aubrey Tucker, and my dad always taught me to stay in the fight until the other person falls. Until those pigs are in jail, I'm staying in the ring. Plus, I'm hoping we'll get to practice today. But, for now, therapy will remain in the back of my mind.

Chapter 8: "The Ultimate Betrayal"

"Mr. and Ms. Tucker, thank you for coming to see us today. Aubrey, I will make sure your teachers allow you to make up any missed work," our headmistress, Mrs. Newman, stated.

"Mrs. Newman, why are we here?" my mom questioned. She was mad that they called this meeting at the last minute. My mom was supposed to meet with a new client today. My dad told her to attend her meeting and he'd fill her in, but she insisted on coming. Now she's annoyed.

"I know you two are busy, but I wanted to update you on the investigation about what was written on Aubrey's locker. I would like first to offer my sympathy about everything. I can't imagine all that she is going through at this age. As parents, I am sure it's hard for you also. I wanted to make sure Aubrey was supported when she returned to school.

"When I saw what happened to her last month, I was angry. My pulse was speeding. My body tensed up, and I felt heat flush through me. I couldn't believe my eyes. I asked Coach Mona to speak with each girl alone. I wanted her to get a feel of their emotions. I requested she ask specific questions. After a month-long investigation, we found out who did it. When we spoke with the two individuals and their parents, they confessed. They have been expelled. We have a zero-tolerance policy on racism. I was surprised when I found out who did it."

"I don't mean to be rude, Mrs. Newman, but can you let us know who did it?" my mom interrupted.

"I understand. It was Emma Watson and Hanna Long."

"Why were you surprised? Hanna's father is a cop. Emma hates me," I spoke up.

"I thought you were friends with Emma," Mrs. Newman inquired.

"At this point, I think who friends with who is irrelevant. Other than expulsion, what else will happen to them? Why did they do it?" my mother asked.

"We can only expel them. I know you would like more, but that's all the school can do. I'm not telling you, but your family can seek other legal action."

"Oh, I know we can. I'll be speaking with my lawyer later today. Are we able to get this information in writing?"

"I can provide you with something that our legal team drafted."

"Thank you. Is that all?" my mother continued to talk.

"Hold up! Why did they do it? You told us you knew why," I interrupted.

"I'm not supposed to say anything, but I believe you should know. Emma did it because she was mad about the whole Allison issue. Emma didn't like how you were treating Allison. She insisted Allison had nothing to do with it. Hanna stated Emma asked her to be the lookout. Hanna's parents told us she's dealing with a lot since her dad is a police officer. She didn't like that your family was going after the police department. I wish things didn't turn out this way. Aubrey, I would like for you to be safe here. If you ever feel like you're being mistreated, let me know. My door is always open."

"Thank you," I replied.

My parents and I walked out Mrs. Newman's office. I went to class, and they both went to work. As I was walking back to class, our lunch bell rang. I saw Bailey in the hall, looking like she had lost her best friend.

"Hey girl, what's wrong?"

"I got a C on my paper for English. My mom is going to be pissed off," Bailey explained.

"It's your first C. I don't think she'll be that mad."

"We're talking about my mom. She's a perfectionist, and anything under an A is unacceptable. Receiving a B is borderline failing. So, you must know what a C is. Of course, it doesn't help that now my dad is back home and he agrees with everything she says."

"I thought your dad was staying with your aunt."

"That didn't last long. My parents were spending too much time together. Plus, my dad got a job at a warehouse with the help of his probation officer. So, now that he can help with bills, he's okay with living there."

"I just realized how much you say the word so."

"My dad said the same thing over the weekend."

"How long will your dad be on parole?"

"Two years. He can't leave the country. If he leaves the state, he needs permission first. I'm glad my dad likes his job. It's one of the few companies that hire ex-felons and pay decently. The only issue is that it's 45 minutes away. He doesn't have his license yet. He has an appointment to have it renewed. My mom said he can use her other car when everything with his license is worked out until he's ready to buy one."

"That's good your dad is getting back on his feet. You guys should come over for dinner one day. I'll ask my parents."

"Umm, your parents are divorced."

"And! My dad hasn't seen your dad in years. I'm sure they would love to catch up."

"If you say so. I'll let you handle that. But, why are you coming from the office?"

"Don't tell anyone, but we found out who wrote on my locker."

"Who the fuck did it? I'm ready to release this anger because of this C."

"It was Emma and Hanna."

"I fucking knew it was Emma. But, Hanna? I am shocked."

"I'm not. She stands with blue. Her dad is a cop."

"I didn't know that, but it makes sense. What happened to them? Did they get detention?"

"Hell no! They both were expelled, and my mom is considering other legal action."

"Yes, Ms. Tessa. Burn those racist ass bitches to the ground," Bailey whispered as she imitated herself flickering a lighter as we walked to our table in the cafeteria.

"You're stupid! What are you doing this weekend? I want to go skating."

"If my parents don't punish me, I'll go. We can go skating and then get something to eat."

"If I don't hear from you tonight, I know your mom put you on lockdown."

"See, you do know my mom. Did you bring your lunch? I'm going to buy a pizza."

"I'm getting some mozzarella sticks and a salad. You know if Coach sees this, she will make practice ten times harder."

"Lucky for us, she's not here during the day. Did they say why those two did what they did, Aubrey?"

"It's not even worth repeating. Two jealous white girls will sum it up. They can't handle this black girl magic dripping throughout this school."

"Facts!"

"Are you ready for the meet tomorrow?"

"I guess. I'm trying to beat my time from our race against Garrison Lake. Coach, was not happy that I finished in 25 minutes. You know, last year, my time was holding around 23 minutes."

"Oh, trust me, I know. I noticed how hard she worked you at practice the next day. Are you okay? It seems like you have been off your game lately. First, running and now the C."

"Sis, I'm good. I told you, with my dad being back home, it's a lot more pressure on me. He's never been to one of my meets, and I just wanted to impress him."

"That's why I think the dinner would be perfect. Let the adults focus on each other and not us. I'm going to ask my mom if Sunday is okay."

***

I knew something wasn't right with Bailey. For weeks she had been acting weird. That C wasn't her first grade below an A. She received a C on her Trig test, but our teacher let her retake it. I'm sure her parents never saw it.

We went skating as planned on Saturday. On Saturdays, the rink is always filled with teens. This day was no different. That's why I wasn't surprised when I saw Jason there. He was there with his friends and some boy who he said was his cousin.

He spoke and introduced Bailey and me to them. None of them went to Liberty Prep, but I did recognize his friend LaQuan from a party I went to last school year. Zyair had a party for his birthday. I was reluctant to go because he was only a freshman, but I went since I knew him from BSU. I remember seeing LaQuan's face there. I still don't know the connection between the three. Zyair and Jason are cool because both are on the basketball team. But, truthfully, LaQuan's presence didn't matter. It was something else that caught my attention.

Bailey was acting differently. Jason spoke to her, and she rolled her eyes. I figured it was because he broke up with me. I left it alone. I was no longer mad at him for breaking up with me. I loved her for the loyalty, but it wasn't needed. Jason and I were cordial. We skated for about three hours before we left to eat. The plan was for Bailey and me to eat together, but a few other people at the rink came along. At first, I didn't want anyone to come with us. It was a girl's day, but we all ended up having fun.

Then Sunday came, and that's when the bombshell was dropped. I asked my parents about having Bailey's parents over for dinner. I thought I would have to convince my dad to come, but he was eager to see Bailey's dad. My dad cooked salmon over rice and asparagus with a side salad. Bailey's mom brought over a lemon pound cake for dessert. Dinner was going great. Our parents were catching up on old times, and we were sitting in the family room watching videos on our phones that our stupid classmates made. That's when we overheard something from Bailey's mom.

"I love that Bailey stayed on top of running since we left Texas. I was afraid she wouldn't stick with it. Bailey was mad that we were leaving Texas. She was close with her friends at her old school. Once I enrolled her back at Liberty Prep, she hadn't skipped a beat until now. At first, I thought her grades were dropping because of practice and senior year jitters. But it was because we found out she was sneaking around seeing some boy named Jason. Bailey was coming home from practice late a few nights. I thought their coach was keeping them later. Her lil ass was spending time at this boy's house. The crazy thing is, his parents were okay with it.

"We don't mind her having a boyfriend. The problem is he's a big distraction, and Bailey is messing up. At first, we told her she could no longer see him. We saw how hurt she was. She likes this boy. We compromised and told her that if she could stop sneaking around and keep up with her grades, she may continue to see him only on the weekend. That was all fine until she brought home a C in Biology. Bailey knows a C does not fly in my house, especially when she wants to be a doctor. You can't be an anesthesiologist and flunking Biology. I told her Friday after their meet; it was over between the two. She came in last place, and I knew it was because of him."

"These damn teenagers," my mom said.

"Wasn't Aubrey seeing some boy named Jason from the school?" my dad mentioned.

"Yeah, she was. But I'm sure it's not the same one," my mom added as they all looked at me, staring at Bailey.

As I sat and listened to her mom talk about how Jason had been distracting Bailey, I didn't say anything. Bailey sat on the couch and stared at me with this dumb look on her face. This year has been betrayal after betrayal—first Allison and now Bailey. Bailey thought somehow that she was different than Allison. She's a bitch just like her. I bet the reason Jason broke up with me didn't have anything to do with his parents. It was because he was fucking the one close friend I had left.

"How could you, Bailey? That's why you were acting like that yesterday," I said as I walked towards the steps to my bedroom.

"I'm sorry, I didn't know. I think we should go," Bailey's mom said.

"Yes, please go. Bailey, I never expected this from you," I yelled from the middle of the stairs.

"Bailey, get your stuff and let's go. How could you do something like this to your best friend? Not today, but you owe Aubrey an apology. Tessa and Kevin, I am so sorry. We will deal with this and make things right. I hope Aubrey is okay."

"We'll talk to Aubrey, and I'm sure they can get past this," my mom lied.

I wasn't going to get past anything. I don't care that Jason cheated or hooked up with someone after we were over. It's Bailey! Whether it was right after or months later, Jason is off-limits. I would have never done anything like that to her. Bailey may not have stood there and watched me get my ass beat, but she broke my heart beyond repair. I went into my room and watched Bailey and her family leave from my bedroom window. I don't know what her mom was saying, but I saw she was pointing her finger at Bailey. Her dad didn't say much during dinner, and from the looks of things, he wasn't saying anything at the moment. I swear I can't wait until I go away for college. I get to meet new people, and hopefully, they won't betray me.

Chapter 9: "I Want to Be A Normal Teenager"

It's been three months since everything went down with Bailey. We spoke a few days later, and she apologized. I could tell Bailey was hurt for going behind my back, but I couldn't trust her. Bailey told me they didn't see each other until after we broke up. Jason's parents didn't tell him to break up with me. Jason was no longer attracted to me. He started to like Bailey and was getting bored with me because I couldn't sneak around with him. He didn't like me having a security detail either. I forgave Bailey, but there were some awkward moments between us. It has taken some time to get to where we are now, but I still love her.

My dad told me not to allow a boy to get in the middle of our friendship. He said that boys don't think about ruining friendships at this age. The only thing they're thinking about is getting in between the legs of girls. Surprisingly, my mom told me not to trust her. I thought she would be the one to convince me to be friends with her. Instead, Bailey's mom kept calling to apologize for her, which eventually changed my mom's mind.

For Christmas, my mom and I went to California to spend time with my godmother, Anika. Aunt Nika moved to Cali three years ago when she got married. Her husband Morris owns a tech start-up business. Morris wasn't going to leave California after they got married, and Aunt Nika wanted to move anyway. She owns a cleaning business that she turned into a franchise when I was in middle school. Nothing was keeping her here. My mom told her we would come for Christmas because they had my god-sister a week before Thanksgiving. We couldn't be there for the birth with everything going on with me.

They have a six-bedroom and four-bathroom house in West Los Angeles. We had our room and the maid catered to us. On top of that, they have an indoor movie theater, mini gym, and a pool outside. It was fun to spend time with my family and shop on Rodeo Drive with my mother's credit card. After we returned, I spent the New Year with my dad at his company's annual dinner party.

Now that cross country is over, I get to focus more on the BSU until spring sports. The bad thing about that is the trial is supposed to start in March. Just before the start of softball season. Cooper will go on trial first and followed by Brickley. The last thing I need is to be focused on a trial. I'll have recruiters coming out for softball. I told my mom that I didn't want to be there outside of when I was called to the stand. I can't afford to miss so many days from school during my senior year. I definitely can't miss practice. The school is aware of the trial starting and will amp up security. For now, I was living my life as a normal teenager and waiting for college acceptance, and looking for a prom dress.

"Aubrey, did you start working on that essay?"

"Ma, I finished it and emailed it to you last night."

"Oh, I haven't checked my personal email. I think you should consider an Ivy League school. You have the grades for it. Plus, you'll have a better chance of getting a scholarship."

"Ma, I don't want to attend an Ivy League. I have been around those people since I started school. I want to be at an HBCU. Let's not act like you and dad don't have thousands saved up to pay for college."

"I know, but I want you to have a good education."

"Really! I can get a good education at an HBCU. Spellman, A&T, FAMU, Hampton, and many more. If I want to become a teacher, HBCUs will be a great option."

"A teacher Aubrey? I thought we talked about medical school."

"No, you talked about medical school. I always wanted to major in education."

"Okay, but you know teachers don't make much money."

"Everything is not about the money. I want to make a difference."

"Aubrey, you know I'll support you in anything you want to do. I am only asking you to reconsider it."

"I know. Is it okay if I go to Bailey's house? Her parents are having dinner for her brother getting into a certification program."

"I didn't know she had a brother."

"Her god-brother moved in with them last year after his mother passed away."

"Are you sure you're okay with hanging out with Bailey? I know you told me you two are good now. But I feel like you keep holding stuff in. This year, a lot happened, and you don't have to accept every apology. You don't have to be strong. Let me and your dad be the strong ones. If you don't want to forgive her, don't."

"Ma, I'm good. Can I go?"

"Sure! Be careful."

I knew my mom had good intentions, but she worried too much. I wonder what she's going to do when I go off to college. She doesn't have a man; outside of me, her career is the focus. I wish this trial were over so she could start dating the doctor. I know they are still talking. If it's not him, she's talking to someone late at night when she thinks I'm sleeping.

When I arrived at Bailey's house, Sean was standing in front of the door with two girls and two other guys. I assume they are his friends because I don't recognize any of them.

"Hey, Sean, where is Bailey?" I asked.

"She's sitting out back with her father, I think," Sean responded.

"What's up, Shorty?" one of his friends asked.

"My name is not Shorty. If you want to know what's up, start by asking my name," I answered as I walked into the house.

"Aubrey, you made it."

"Bailey, who are those guys outside with Sean?"

"His dirty friends. Girl, don't even look their way. Each of them has a girlfriend and a side chick."

"I was wondering because one of them called me shorty."

"Let me guess. It was Troy, the tall one with the bald head?"

"Yeah, how did you know it was him?"

"He's always trying to talk to someone. Troy tried to holler at me when Sean first started staying here. He tried to talk to my cousin Kamari also. He doesn't have a job. Troy is a momma's boy. From what Sean told my dad, his grandfather died earlier this year and left him over $100,000.00 from a life insurance policy because he was his only grandchild. This dude quit his job and has been living off that money since. And his mother is okay with it."

"I wasn't going to talk to him. I only wanted to know who he was, but thanks for the heads up. Is there anyone else here?"

"It's just us. His friends weren't supposed to come. Sean only asked if he could invite his girlfriend, Gabby. After my mother said yeah, today, these other fools show up. My mother went to get more food, and my dad is upstairs watching television while those dummies are standing outside in the cold."

"Is one of those girls Gabby?"

"No. Gabby, well, Gabrielle may not make it. He met her in college, and her parents would not allow her to drive to Maryland alone. Her mom offered to bring her, but Gabby said no because her parents didn't know Sean was black. Sean is her little secret."

"Is he okay with that, Bailey?"

"I guess so. The only thing this proves is Gabby is from a racist ass family, and we don't trust her. My mom keeps telling him to leave her alone, but he thinks he knows everything."

***

"Did you enjoy dinner, Aubrey? I know it's not your father's cooking," Mrs. Stephanie said.

"Everything was good. I loved the chicken salad."

"Don't be lying to her, Aubrey," Mr. Dwayne joked.

"Babe, you know I can cook."

"No, everything was good. I promise you."

"Come on, Aubrey, let's go back upstairs to my room," Bailey instructed.

"Aubrey, what time is your mom expecting you to be back home?" Mrs. Stephanie asked.

"I have to be home by 11, but I already text her."

"Okay! Bailey, your dad and I are going to the movies. Sean probably won't be back until later tonight."

"Ma, how did you two fix dinner for him but he leaves as soon as they finish eating. What do the old folks say? Eat and run!"

"Well, no one over here is old. Sean is an adult, and I know he appreciated the dinner. He's still dealing with the death of his mother. Take it easy on him."

"I know, but I'm just saying. Come on, Aubrey."

***

"Remember Aubrey; they will try to discredit you when you're on the stand. I know it'll be hard but don't let them upset you," Mrs. Pamela told me.

The officer's trial will be starting next week. Since I left Bailey's house that night, I tried to keep myself occupied. I hung out with Bailey a lot. Either she was at my house, or I was at hers. Everyone is trying to prepare me for the day. I know reliving that day will bring up a lot of anger, but I need to do this. My mom told the school I would not be there during the day. I thought this would cause me not to be able to practice. If I do my work at home, I can still practice. My mother asked my teachers to email my work over with a deadline.

On top of dealing with this trial, Jason and Allison reached out to me. Jason was calling me, but I ignored every call. Until one day, I received a call from Zyair. At least I thought it was him. Jason was calling from his phone. When I found out it was him, I wanted to hang up, but I didn't. He apologized for everything.

"Jason, what do you want?"

"Aubrey, I messed up. I didn't want Bailey. She came on to me."

"I don't believe you. Bailey told me what happened. She's my girl, and I know she wouldn't lie to me."

"She's not who you think she is. Shorty is thirsty."

"What about when you lied and said your parents told you not to see me?"

"That's in the past. What are you trying to do? Are you trying to see me this weekend? My parents won't be here."

"Jason, I'm not coming over to your house. My mother is not going to let me. She knows what you did."

"Shit, tell her you're going to Bailey's house. We don't have to do anything; I just want to see you. If you're worried, my granny does live here. She'll be here with us."

"I don't know, Jason. I can't trust you."

"I feel like you're putting all of the blame on me. Bailey messed up too, but you're still friends with her. Come on! I miss you. I know you miss me."

"Jason, I don't know."

"I have to go. Text me before we get out of school on Friday. If I don't hear from you, I'll know not to fuck with you. Bye."

Before I could say anything, Jason hung up the phone. The next day I saw Jason after I left practice and told him I was still thinking about it. He didn't say anything. Jason walked to his car and pulled off. Here I am, sitting in the living room, wondering if I should lie to my mother. I just came in from practice. My mom told me she would be getting home later than usual. I want to go, but my only dilemma is the security team sitting outside. I can't tell my mother I'm going to Bailey's because they know where she lives. My phone ringing pulled me out of the lie I planned to tell.

"Hey, Ma."

"Aubrey, order something to eat for dinner. Use my credit card that's on my dresser. I probably won't be home until after midnight. It's tax season, and you know how that goes. With the trial being next week, I don't want to fall behind."

"What happened to you not working past a certain time?"

"I know, but I have to get these taxes submitted."

"Okay. Can Mr. Shawn go home?"

"Why? You know they are to be there at all times."

"I figured I would eat and go to sleep."

"Aubrey, you already know the answer. Order your food and chill. It's Friday night."

"Okay. I'll see you when you get back."

Since I couldn't leave, I would let Jason come here. I had a plan, but I needed to make sure it would work.

"Yo, I didn't think you would call."

"I was trying to figure out how I would see you. I can't leave the house because my mom is working late. Plus, my security team is here. I do have an idea."

"What's your plan?"

"I'll sneak you in here. Come over but park a few doors up. I'm going to call my security in, and then I'll text you to go around my back. I'll let you in once he goes back outside."

"Hell no! Yo, I'm a black boy sneaking around your house. You live in a white neighborhood."

"Trust me. You can come through the basement door. I'll unlock it, but you have to make sure you close the door quietly. My mom won't be home until around midnight."

"What about when I leave? Your security team will see me leaving."

"Shit, I didn't think about that."

"Right."

"Or, I can tell my mother to let me know when she gets home so I can tell security to keep an eye out for her. Then when I know she's close, I will call him in, and you can go out the back door."

"Say less. Let me know when you want me to come."

I knew I was going against the rules, but I wanted to see Jason. I ordered my food and set my plan in motion. Jason sent me a text letting me know he was on my street. I went to the front door and waved to Mr. Shawn to come in. My food was going to be about another 30 minutes.

"Hey Aubrey, is everything okay?"

"Yes. Did my mom call you?"

I'm glad it wasn't bright at 7:30 because Jason slipped past Mr. Shawn to my backyard.

"Yeah, she told me she'll be late coming in."

"Oh, okay. I just wanted to make sure you'll keep an eye out for her when she comes in."

"I am about to leave. Austin will be here in about 40 minutes for the night shift. I'll be sure to let him know your mom will be in late."

"Thanks. Oh, it looks like my food is here."

"All right, Aubrey. Have a good night."

As Mr. Shawn walked back to his car, the delivery driver gave me my salad and left. I locked the door and turned the alarm on. I made sure I switched the backyard camera off before calling Mr. Shawn to the door. When he walked away and locked the door, I flipped the switch back on. If my mother questions it, I'll tell her I flipped the wrong switch. It is right next to the light switch. I put my salad in the refrigerator because I wasn't hungry. It was part of my excuse to get Jason in the house. I went down into the basement and saw Jason sitting on the couch.

"Why didn't you turn the television on?"

"Shit, I didn't want that big ass motherfucker to hear me down here."

"Well, I sent my mother a text to see if she wanted me to order her something. She told me not to worry about it because she probably wouldn't be back until after midnight. She didn't want to bring any work home."

"That means I have a little more time with you. I miss you."

"I miss you too, Jason. So, what's up? Why did you want to see me?"

"I told you I missed you, shorty."

"Do you want to watch a movie?"

"Yeah, that's cool."

I turned on the television and started flipping through the channels. Just before I could ask Jason what he wanted to watch, he leaned over and kissed me. This wasn't the first time I kissed someone. But this was the first time it was in my house. Jason and I kissed many times before, but things felt different this time. I had never had sex. I wasn't saving myself for marriage. I never found anyone that I wanted to have sex with. At this moment, I wondered if Jason could be the one as he started rubbing my thighs.

Jason leaned in even more, which caused me to lay back on the couch. Finally, he got on top of me, and I knew exactly what was going through his mind. I could tell by what was poking me in between my legs.

"Have you ever had sex before?" Jason whispered in my ear.

"No," I mumbled.

"Do you want to?" he asked as he talked in between, kissing my neck.

"Jason, I don't know."

"That's cool. We don't have to. We can keep doing this. Are you okay with that?"

"Yeah, I like it."

As Jason continued to kiss me, he started to ease his fingers down my leggings. I wanted him to stop, but I knew what he was trying to do. A big part of me wanted to know how it would feel for someone to touch me like that. I thought about losing my virginity tonight. Jason made a mistake with Bailey. If I could forgive her, why couldn't I do the same with him?

"Lift up, Jason"

Jason sat up, and I pulled my t-shirt over my head. Jason's eyes got really big. He pulled his shirt over his head and laid back on top of me. I was sure this was going to be it. Until the worst thing that could have happened, happened.

"Aubrey Simone Tucker, what the hell do you think you're doing?" my mom yelled.

Jason jumped up and grabbed his shirt. I lay there in shock because she was home early. I was embarrassed.

"And who are you?"

"Ma, this is Jason?"

"He can speak for himself. The same boy who went after your best friend because he was in his feelings. You have him in my house doing what?"

"We were just kissing Ma."

"It looks like you two were about to do more than just kissing. You're half-dressed in my basement. Lil boy, do your parents knows where you are?"

"No, ma'am. They they they are not home," Jason stuttered.

"I suggest you put your shirt on and go home."

"Are you going to call his parents?"

"He's not my child. I don't need to call his parents about anything. I need him to get out of my house."

Jason didn't say anything. He put his shirt on, grabbed his jacket, and headed towards the back door.

"Uh, no! You're leaving out through the front door. Aubrey, get dressed, and I will meet you upstairs."

My mom and Jason walked up the basement steps, and I was horrified. I was caught with a boy in my house. If my mom hadn't walked in, we would have had sex. I'm glad she only caught us kissing. I heard the front door close, and I crept up the steps.

"I don't know why you're moving up the steps so slow. Bring your ass up here and have a seat."

"Ma, I'm sorry."

"Aubrey, how did he get in here? What were you thinking?"

"I told Jason to park a few doors up. I called Mr. Shawn to the house and pretended to ask him questions. Jason snuck around back. I left the door open for him."

"Aubrey, why would you want the same guy over here that tried to get with your best friend? Are you having sex?"

"I never had sex before."

"Were you planning to have sex with him tonight?"

"At first, no. But once he started kissing me, I wanted to know how it would feel. Are you going to tell dad?"

"Yes, I am. You already know your friends are not allowed in the house without my permission. Then you snuck a boy that treated you like trash into my house. I can't even talk to you right now. Get out of my face."

***

I woke up the next morning hearing my mother on the phone telling someone what I had done. I don't know who she was talking to, but my mom was loud and sounded like she was still pissed. I checked my phone before I went into my bathroom, and there was a text from my dad telling me to call him when I woke up.

I put off calling my dad. After showering, I went downstairs to eat breakfast and apologize to my mom. When I went to the kitchen, my mom was done with her call and was now in her office on her laptop.

"Good morning. Can we talk?"

"What do you need, Aubrey?"

"Ma, I'm sorry for having Jason over last night. I know it wasn't the right thing to do."

"Aubrey, what made you want to see him again? He tried to get with your best friend. Well, he did get with her."

"I'm not even going to lie. He started calling me again, but I would ignore him. One day he called me from Zyair's phone. He told me Bailey was a liar, and I started questioning her friendship in the back of my mind. He asked me to come over to his house. I knew whoever was on duty would have followed me, so I told him to come here."

"I don't know what to say. We have so much going on right now. Your focus should be on this trial and not some dusty ass boy who would dump you at the drop of a dime."

"Am I punished?"

"No. What's the point in punishing you? You're seventeen years old, and even if I punish you, you'll sneak and see him. Your father and I have always taught you about respecting yourself. You allowed this boy to disrespect you last night. You were going to have sex with him, and he's not even your boyfriend. Did you have a condom?"

"No."

"So, you were going to lose your virginity to a boy without a condom? What about diseases and pregnancy?"

"Ma, I don't think he has anything."

"Aubrey, you can't be that stupid. Obviously, what I'm saying and have always told you is not resonating with you right now. I will let your father deal with you. I suggest you call him back and stop trying to prolong it. He'll be here later to take you out."

***

My dad took me out to lunch. I was prepared for him to yell at me, but he didn't. What he did tell me was Jason was playing me. That's all he said outside of him telling me to think about everything Jason has done to me in the past year. I knew my dad was right, but Jason was my first boyfriend. I also knew I was smarter than this. I didn't want to believe I was being played until Bailey sent me a text asking if I needed to tell her something. Then she sent me a screenshot of Jason texting her.

"I told you your girl was trying to get with me. She invited me to her house."

I couldn't believe Jason had told her. I knew I messed up. I didn't know what to say to Bailey, so I waited until I got home to call her. When my dad dropped me off, he told me I was punished. I was a bit confused because my mom told me I wasn't. I couldn't drive my car for a week. The security team had to drive me everywhere. I wasn't happy about it, but the punishment was small compared to what could have happened.

"Ma, I'm back."

"How did your talk with your father go?"

"He told me I couldn't drive my car for a week."

"Good. I am supposed to go out tonight. I trust that you are capable of staying home alone without sneaking someone into my house. Or, do I need to drop you off at Grand-Grand's house?"

"I promise I will not let anyone in. I have homework to do. Plus, I need to call Bailey and explain everything. Jason told her he was over here."

"That's why you can't trust these lil boys. Keep your head in the books and away from boys. You're about to go to college. Trust me; you'll have plenty of boys in your face."

"Yes, ma'am. Where are you going?"

"I am going on a date with Dr. Chambers."

"I thought you two weren't going public."

"We're not. I'm going to his house for dinner."

"Okay."

"And by the way, you don't owe Bailey an explanation."

My mom was right. I didn't owe Bailey an explanation, especially after what she did to me. But she's my friend, and I didn't want to keep any more secrets. I called Bailey three times, and the phone rang once and went to voicemail. I figured either she was busy or ignoring me. If Bailey were busy, she would have sent me a text message. Most likely, it's the ignoring part. If that's the case, it's cool. She doesn't have the room to do so since she fucked me over first.

I pulled out my laptop and started working on some homework. I only had a few more months left in school. I picked my college, prom was approaching, and our softball team was good enough to go to the championship. Those things weren't even the highlight of my senior year. I had a trial coming up, and the fear was starting to kick in. For the past week, news outlets have been talking about this being the trial of the year. Most said the officers didn't do anything wrong, and someone needed to protect them. Others said I lied about the whole thing, and my mom paid off the witnesses that came forth. My dad was painted as a deadbeat and cheater. The only people on my side are those who look like me. Well, some of them. My parents keep telling me not to look at the news or social media. I can't help it.

I sat in bed staring at my assignment on my laptop screen for who knows how long. I woke up around eight the next morning. After going into the bathroom, I went to my mom's room to ask about her date, but I stopped before knocking on the door. I overheard her talking to who I expected was my dad.

"I wish you had my back about making sure Aubrey attends therapy regularly."

"I understand what you are saying, Kevin, but something is wrong with her. She's sneaking boys into the house. Aubrey has never done anything like this before."

"Yeah, I know. I just don't want her to get caught up in some bullshit behind this punk ass boy. And I don't trust Bailey."

"Okay. Call Aubrey when you get off and talk to her. Please."

I wish I could have heard what my dad was saying. Did he think I was losing it like my mother? I walked back to my room and closed the door. I messed up one time, and now something's wrong with me. I know my mom messed up as a teen. I guess she was used to me being so perfect, like how she groomed me. Now that I was stepping out and living my own life, I needed help. College was my focus point to get away from everything and everyone.

***

Today is the end of Cooper's trial. The verdict is supposed to come in later today. I haven't been in school all week. I wanted to go, but my lawyer thought it would help if I were in court so the jury could see me. Brickley's trial will start next Tuesday, and that's the one I fear the most. He scared me more than Cooper. I believe if he weren't there, this would have never happened.

Of course, there were a lot of officers in the courtroom. Jennifer and her husband were there supporting Cooper. It was very intimidating, but Pamela told us that's how it would be. My grandmother, a few neighbors, my mom and dad's friends, some cousins, and surprisingly my step-mother were there. I felt the love and support from everyone. Bailey wanted to come, but my mom thought it would be best for her to attend school. I think it was more because she no longer trust her. We ended up talking about everything, and our issue with Jason is resolved. Now I'm sitting in the café across the street from the courthouse with my family, waiting for someone to call us.

"Come on. Pamela called and said the verdict is in," my mom said.

My dad paid the bill, and we walked over to see what was next. As soon as we reached the courtroom door, two officers stood there. The looks they gave us were as if they wanted us to die right on the spot. We entered the room, and Cooper was sitting next to her attorney with this pitiful look on her face. With Mrs. Wolfe's doorbell camera, there was no way Cooper could lie about anything. We sat in the courtroom for about 10 minutes before the jury came out.

"Will the jury please rise? Will the defendant also please rise and face the jury? Madam Forelady, have your jury reached a verdict? Judge Maxwell asked.

"Yes!"

"What say you, Madam Forelady, as to complaint number 2347, wherein the defendant is charged with second-degree assault, falsifying a report, and harassment, is she guilty or not guilty?"

"We, the jury, find the defendant guilty."

Suddenly, there were mixed reactions in the courtroom. Cooper faked as if she was fainting, but the judge gave her the side-eye, and she straightened up.

"Guilty of what?"

"We find the defendant guilty of second-degree assault and falsifying a report. We find the defendant not guilty of harassment."

After the verdict was read, everything else was like blah, blah, blah. I heard the judge state sentencing would take place in two weeks. Cooper was taken in the back in handcuffs. I was relieved. Pamela immediately had my security detail escort us out of the courtroom because she didn't trust how the officers would react.

Chapter 10: "It's Over, I Think"

Today is the first day of Brickley's trial. I didn't want to miss another day of school. Pamela told my mom that I only needed to come on the day I had to testify, which was day two. When I came to school this morning, I received mixed looks from not only students but also the staff. Of course, Bailey and my other friends from BSU had my back. Even some white students hugged me and told me how they were there for me. When I saw Allison, she would only stare as if she wanted to say something. I ignored her and kept going to wherever I was headed.

I sat at the table with my usual crew during lunchtime, and Allison walked over. Like, she had the balls to come and request that we talk.

"Excuse me, Aubrey, can we talk?" Allison requested.

"No!" Bailey responded before I could say anything.

"I'm asking Aubrey."

"Girl, I'm not the one. Don't get fucked up. Aubrey doesn't have anything to say to you," Bailey said.

I was laughing on the inside because Allison's face was turning red. I decided to cool things off because the last thing we needed was more drama.

"Bailey, it's cool. What do you want, Allison?"

"Can we talk in private, please?"

"No. This is my lunchtime. If you want to speak with me, you'll have to make it happen while I eat with my friends."

"It's kind of private."

"Whatever you tell me, I'm going to go back and tell them. What do you want?"

"Okay! I'm sorry for ruining our friendship. You were my best friend; I should have stepped up when you needed me. I also wanted to let you know with everything going on, my family will be leaving Maryland. My mom is moving us to New York. You don't have to worry about seeing me again after our senior year."

"I didn't plan on seeing you anyway. Is that all?"

"No, that's not all. I could have done something to save you, and I didn't. I'm sorry, and I hope you can forgive me."

"Okay."

"So, are you going to accept my apology? I don't want this hanging over my head anymore."

"See, that's that white savior shit. You're feeling guilty about your lies. This could have been resolved long ago, but you and your mom decided to lie. I don't need you or any other white person saving me. The jury saw the evidence and found the officer guilty. Now we just have to wait for that racist Brickley to be convicted. What I would have really liked is for your lying ass mother to be fired and placed on trial with her crew. If that's all, you can go."

"Aubrey, things don't have to be like this. I know we'll never be friends again, but you don't have to be so mean. This isn't like you."

"Oh, so you thought I would stay the same after being beaten by two cops? My arm was broken, multiple bruises on my face and abdomen, and my jaw was broken. I went through months of physical therapy. For a while, I couldn't even eat solid food. I have been dealing with this for exactly one year. Why would I remain the same, Aubrey? This is the new and improved Aubrey, and I don't have anything else to say to you. Goodbye!"

Allison walked away like a typical white woman who wants sympathy from everyone. She had fake tears in her eyes. That caused her friends to console her. I continued eating my lunch and told my friends I didn't want to talk about it.

After lunch was over, I received a text from my mother. She told me that everything was going fine until Brickley's wife had multiple outbursts and the judge had her removed. I'm glad I wasn't there. Today was my first day of softball practice in a while. My coach understands everything, but I hate missing practice. I was ready to go home so my mother could tell me all about the trial.

***

"Ma, how was court today? Did they put Brickley on the stand?"

"No, he's not questioned until tomorrow. That's why no one could figure out why his wife had a loud outburst. Mrs. Wolfe testified again, and the ER front desk clerk. I guess that's what the title is. Pamela questioned her about what happened when you were brought in and the paperwork. There was nothing spectacular about today. Are you ready for tomorrow?"

"Yes. I will be glad when all of this is over."

"It will be soon."

"Was Madison there again today?"

"Yeah. We all went to lunch afterward. We were done around one, and your dad asked me if I wanted to go out for lunch with them. I said no, but Madison practically begged me."

"Did Grand-Grand go?"

"Absolutely not! Your father invited her, and she told him no. She got in her car and drove away."

"So, how did lunch go?"

"It was okay. I didn't do much talking. I was checking work emails the whole time while Madison was running her mouth. I don't even know what she was talking about. I only heard her say, 'girl, we should do this more often.' I grinned and told your father I had to leave for a work conference call."

"You have a new best friend."

"Don't play with me. What do you want for dinner?"

"You're not cooking?"

"Aubrey, I'm not cooking anything after the day I had."

"It doesn't matter. Whatever you want, I'll eat."

***

The day was finally here. We were going to find out if Brickey would be charged. The day I testified was brutal. His lawyer was evil. She was nothing like Cooper's attorney. Both attorneys accused me of doing drugs because of Jason. But this lady questioned my family about being racist towards Allison. Supposedly, Allison never felt comfortable around my family, which is why she always invited me to her house. It was all lies. She revealed that I went through a period of depression after my parents were divorced and how I would drink alcohol when I went to Allison's house. I was shocked when she said it because no one knew about that except for Allison.

I drank twice at her house, and that was it. This lady also mentioned when I revealed to Allison that I thought about committing suicide by taking pills because I thought the divorce was my fault. I saw the pain on my parent's faces. She claimed it was mentioned to show the jury that I was unstable and was probably drunk or high the day everything happened.

My mom didn't say anything to me after court. My dad took me out to dinner so we could talk. I explained that it was the past and nothing was wrong with me. I didn't want to bring up the past, and my dad didn't want to pressure me. I did tell him that for some time, I believed it was my fault they were divorcing. The only reason I confided in Allison was that her parents divorced also. I assured my father I only thought about taking the pills, but I didn't go through with it. He believed me and told me I could always talk to him.

When I got home, my mother had nothing but questions. I feel like she sat in her office while I was with my dad, writing down questions to ask me. As soon as I walked in the door, the questions started.

"Aubrey, would you like to talk about what happened today?"

"Ma, I'm sorry I didn't tell you how I felt. I'm okay. There's nothing to talk about."

"Did you blame yourself? Why didn't you come to me?"

"I did blame myself like most children do when their parent divorce. I no longer blame myself. It was all Madison, and I know that now."

"Aubrey, how many times did you go to Allison's house to drink? Where did you get the pills from? Was the alcohol her mother's? Did she know you two were drinking?"

"Ma, please stop with all of the questions. The two times we were drinking together weren't about the divorce. The first time, Allison had a party, and one of the girls wanted to play truth or dare, which involved drinking. The second time, her older cousin stayed with them for a while. She was in the basement drinking one day and offered some to us. I took one shot, and that was it. I don't know what Allison told this lawyer, but the drinking incident didn't have anything to do with the divorce.

"I did confide in her that I thought about taking some pills. I didn't want to kill myself, but I figured it would get you and daddy's attention. I only thought about it. I didn't even have any pills. Ma, I am okay. Trust me."

"I still think you should go back to therapy. I know you don't want to, but something is going on with you."

"Ma, I don't need therapy. I need for this trial to be over. I want you to trust me and believe me when I say that chapter in my life is over. I no longer blame myself. Yes, I would love to see you two together again. But I am old enough to know it will not happen."

"If you say so. I am here if you ever need me."

After that conversation, my mom left me alone for the rest of the night. When I woke up this morning, she had breakfast ready and an outfit picked out for me. My mom hadn't picked out my clothes since I was in middle school. I didn't want to debate with her, so I gave in. If picking out my clothes would stop her from hovering over me about the alcohol and pills, I'm keeping my mouth closed.

My dad and the rest of the family met us at the courthouse. Pamela wanted us there by 9 to go over different scenarios. If he was found guilty, everything was fine. She wanted to prepare us for the back lash if he was found not guilty. We would have to go through this all over again if it were a mistrial.

We arrived at court, and the media was everywhere. Microphones were pushed in our faces trying to get a comment from us. Mr. Shawn and Mr. Denny guided us through the crowd. They wouldn't allow anyone to speak with us. We finally reached the inside, and it was no better than the outside. Police officers were everywhere, offering us dirty looks. My mother, dad, and I met Pamela behind closed doors to discuss everything.

We entered the courtroom, and surprisingly, Jennifer was there. She hadn't shown up for Brickley's trial until today. The judge came in. The jury was called in, and everything after that was a blur. After the jury was brought in, I only remember two not guilty and one guilty verdict. Brickley was found guilty on one charge, falsifying a report. I didn't care anything about the report. He should have been charged with assault. But, what did I expect when I looked at the jury filled with eight white men, two white women, one black woman, and one Asian man? He was free to go, and Cooper was going to jail.

Mr. Shawn and Mr. Denny took us out of the courthouse through the backdoor. My parents and Madison didn't drive their cars. We rode inside Mr. Shawn's truck. Mr. Denny picked my dad and Madison up from their place that morning. The rest of my family went out through the front of the courthouse. We were all upset, but there was nothing we could do about it. Pamela met us at the house to talk about what happened. I didn't want to hear anything. Instead, I went to my room, took a shower, and laid down.

I don't know why I did that because now my mother was trying to talk to me through the door. I came out of my room because she wanted me to speak with Pamela about the next moves.

"Aubrey, I know today didn't go as planned. I'm sorry, but this is not over. I spoke with your parents, and we are still moving forward with the civil lawsuit against the county and police department. They had already offered a settlement, but your parents thought it was a good idea to put it on hold until after the verdict. All parties agreed. I don't know if Brickley will lose his job or not, but I do know they are tired of the bad press," Pamela explained.

"I don't care anything about the money. I don't think it's fair that Cooper was charged and not him. He initiated everything. I don't understand why the jury didn't see that," I stated.

"He's a white man in white America," my dad said.

"Listen, everyone, I know we are all disappointed with the verdict, but this is still a win. Cooper will be sentenced on Tuesday. Brickley should have been found guilty, but we can still get him fired. If that happens, he will lose his pension. Either way, he's out. Let me move forward with the civil suit."

"It's up to my parents. I don't care. I have some homework to catch up on."

I walked away from their conversation. I no longer cared about any of it. It was time to finish the school year, enjoy my summer, and go to college. I am ready to get away from everything and everyone in Maryland.

***

My senior year didn't turn out the way I planned. But as a black woman, will anything ever go as planned for me. Cooper was sentenced to five years in prison with the possibility of parole in two. That was some bullshit. Brickley wasn't fired for falsifying the report. Instead, they took his gun away, and he was placed on desk duty. The civil lawsuit is still pending because no one can decide on a dollar amount.

Graduation day came, and I was finally closing this chapter of my life. I thought my graduation day would be something spectacular, but it wasn't. We walked across the stage and heard a bunch of speeches about how our life will change. I thought I would be valedictorian, but I wasn't. This guy named Norman was, and he deserved it. We both had a 4.0 GPA, but the only thing that messed me up was my community service. He had 50 more hours than I did. I wasn't valedictorian, but I did get the title of Salutatorian.

Per the gossip mill in my neighborhood, Allison and her family did move back to New York a few weeks after we graduated. I'm glad I'll never see her again.

I was accepted into every school that I applied to. I received a full scholarship to five of them. I picked my number one choice in Virginia. Hampton University. I won't be too far away from home but far enough. I will finally be able to be Aubrey Simone Tucker again, at least I hope so.

"So, Aubrey, how does it feel to finally tell your story?" my therapist asked.

"I don't know. A new chapter is about to start and I have a feeling I'll be telling it again."